Restoring Christmas

Julie Arduini

978-1-7336876-2-1

Cover created by Surrendered Scribe Media, photos courtesy Lizz Clark, Shutterstock.com, Pixabay.com
Published by Surrendered Scribe Media, Youngstown, Ohio, 44514

http://juliearduini.com

A Message for Readers:

Restoring Christmas first appeared in the October 2018 boxed set, *A Christmas to Remember.*

Dedication:

I dedicate this to my Heavenly Father, who through Jesus restored my love of Christmas. This is also for anyone who struggles with the holidays. There is healing through Christ's love.

Chapter One

If Holly Christmas' heart was in charge, returning to Geneseo Valley never would have happened. She slowed her Subaru Forester and blinked away fresh tears. The car shook as Holly wavered between the brake and accelerator. If memories alone could steer, the car would be parked in the lot she had played in since she could walk.

With her uncle expecting her, she cruised into the parking area adjacent to the family business. Holly found a space to stop thanks to faded yellow lines. Dabbing her eyes and cheeks with a tissue, she grabbed her planner, slung her purse over her shoulder, and got out. With a deep breath, she faced the historic mansion ahead of her.

The crunch of late September leaves marked her tentative steps toward the main entrance. Glancing ahead, she noted the overgrown weeds and bushes out front in desperate need of a pruning. The once red and white striped pole showed rust spots and the red faded to pink. The sign that once proudly displayed the tourist destination was now a rotted piece of splinter. The engraving was more of a petri dish for moss and algae, making it barely readable.

Welcome to Christmas Mansion.

Holly stopped, a shudder zigzagged from head to toe. Regaining her balance, she kept her focus on the cement steps as she sidestepped a jagged chunk in the path. The porch still featured the wooden soldier she stood next to every year to mark how much she'd grown. The stiff greeter was a shell of his former holiday glory, nearly as faded as everything else. She opened the almost pink colored door and sighed at the sound of a sinister squeak. *This isn't the Christmas Mansion. It's a Halloween spook house.*

Fighting the urge to run back to her car and her life in Ohio, Holly cleared her throat. "Uncle Nick? It's Holly. Are you here?"

She glanced around the lobby, the same register with a bell sound she pushed as a teen after a customer purchase. Dusty shelves housed a potpourri of holiday items—candles, snow globes, and ornaments thrown together in complete chaos.

Before she could investigate further, a shuffle echoed from the hallway and her uncle entered. "Holly? I can't believe it, right here in Upstate New York. What an answer to prayer." The cobalt blue glint in his eyes reminded her of her father.

She stepped into her uncle's hug, surprised by his emotion as he held onto her arms and gazed into her eyes. "I don't know about answer to prayer, but things changed with my job, and I thought it was a good time to help out." She waved her hands with animation. "Here I am!"

The younger Christmas brother nodded. "I've tried to keep things going after your father passed, but I can't even fit into his Santa suit."

Holly smiled as she glanced at his thin frame. "A few cookies from Mrs. Olson will take care of that." The volunteer greeter was a Geneseo Valley legend for her sugar cookies.

His smile disappeared. "You didn't hear? Mrs. Olson passed in July. That's one of the many things I need to do—find a new greeter. Then there's a landscaping team. I know it's September, but it won't be long until school kids visit." He scratched his balding head. "I did take care of one thing. I arranged for a group from a local school to get the gift shop back in order. Your father was so beloved as Chris Christmas that everyone seemed to overlook the haphazard way he organized the shop."

Holly attempted to tame the rolling waves in her stomach. Mrs. Olson was a Christmas Mansion staple as much as her father was all about dressing up as Santa and entertaining. Her grin didn't last long. She didn't need to tour the mansion to know the entire place was a mess. The financial state most likely wasn't much better. "Great. The students will have their work cut out for them. I still have unpacking to do at the house, but the place still opens at eight on weekdays, right?"

Uncle Nick hesitated. "Yes, but…"

She fished the keys out of her purse. "Great. I'll be ready to start tomorrow." Before she could find her sunglasses, the front door burst open and a choir of adolescent chatter filled the lobby. Kids who looked to be around junior high age swarmed the area, pointing at the shelves and leaning on the glass case that housed the register. "Uncle Nick?"

Before he could speak, among the chaos emerged a man with a red and black plaid flannel shirt. His wavy black locks bobbed as he whistled. All the students froze and focused on him with the same intensity Holly gave. The mesmerizing stranger pulled out his phone, opened a screen, and traced his finger down the screen before looking up. "Hi. I'm supposed to meet with a Nick Christmas?"

Kevin resisted the urge to pull out his black-rimmed glasses from his shirt pocket. It was hard enough to keep the students' attention without putting on the eyewear that made the group of children with slight special needs call him Clark Kent. If only he felt like Superman.

A senior citizen with a friendly smile stepped forward, his hand extended. "That's me. Is this the group from Geneseo Valley Central School?"

The gentleman's handshake was firm, and he looked Kevin in the eye. To Nick's side stood a woman who looked about his age, gorgeous hair the same midnight-black shade as his, her mouth slightly open as she watched. "I'm Kevin Holt. I'm a Special Ed teacher at the school, and I supervise projects for the community." He chuckled. "The Christmas Mansion is our latest endeavor."

A fidgety boy blurted, "Do we get to be elves?"

Giggles bounced off the walls that featured spots of peeling paint. He stole a glance at the woman. She didn't move, but her eyes darted across the room. "You know, Kensi, I'm not sure. We're here for the tour so we know what to expect when we come next time to work."

The woman shifted and faced Mr. Christmas. "Uncle Nick, what's going on?"

He patted her hand. "Holly, this was the last piece of business your dad conducted before he died. This is the group of students who are going to help get the gift shop in shape, and whatever else you come up with. They have some special circumstances, so Mr. Holt has them help out businesses to build their skills and confidence."

Kevin noted her tight smile as Nick grabbed a falling snow globe a student fumbled. Kevin's pulse quickened. Whether it was stress, or Holly's ebony curls, he wasn't sure. "They are good kids. A little active today because it's our first field trip of the year."

He glanced over at the table with a pile of wreaths. His best friend's son, Nathan Welling, had one in hand, ready to use it as a frisbee. Kevin scurried over and plucked the greenery away, but the busy child wasn't finished.

Nathan cocked his head to the side, eyeing Holly. He squinted, then nodded. "You work here?"

Holly fidgeted. "I co-own Christmas Mansion."

Nathan crossed his arms and shook his head. "You can't!"

Kevin wanted to place a firm hand over the child's mouth.

Holly fired back with her own narrow stare. "And why not?"

Nathan didn't waste a moment. "You hate Christmas.

Chapter Two

Holly lagged behind the tour group to move snow globes to a higher shelf and process what the boy with a mean cowlick said. She didn't dare glance at Uncle Nick after the boy's declaration, and thankfully the teacher with admirable biceps insisted they begin.

Before she could place the last globe in its new home, the boy appeared beside her. "Aren't you coming?"

Holly quickly rid herself of the glass before she dropped it, and faced the child. "Are you allowed to leave the group?"

He shrugged. "I wanted to check on you."

Holly felt her fragile heart for the first time since her father passed. "Thanks. What's your name?"

"Nathan. You look sad."

She gulped and forced her hands to her side so they wouldn't shake. Or, that he wouldn't notice. "Nathan, it's nice to meet you. I'm Miss Christmas. I guess I'm kind of sad, but mostly overwhelmed."

He picked up a candy cane shaped pen and twirled it. "For real, your name is Christmas? That's cool. Why are you sad?"

She took a breath and was about to answer when the muscular teacher appeared, this time wearing black frame glasses that made her heart beat faster than the rhythm to *Jingle Bells*.

The man ran a hand through his thick, wavy black hair. "Nathan, you aren't allowed to leave the group. Let's go. I'm sorry, Miss. He shouldn't be bothering you."

Holly's focus darted between the two. "No, it's fine. He was making sure I was okay. It was sweet. I could join the tour, it's been awhile since I've been here."

Nathan started to open his mouth, but the man shot him a look, and the boy remained silent. The trio walked past the first stop, the adjoining room to the gift shop where the Christmas tree proudly stood. Holly spotted Uncle Nick and the others examining the St. Nicholas collection from different years and countries.

The teacher jogged ahead. "Boys and girls, make sure you don't touch anything unless Mr. Christmas says so."

Nathan chuckled and looked to Holly. "The grocery store didn't ask us back after we played catch with the pickle jars."

She stifled a smile as the two stepped closer to the others. "Nathan, why did you say I hate Christmas?"

His face scrunched as if she asked the most ridiculous question in the world. "Next to Disney, this should be the happiest place in the world. It's all about Christmas. You don't even smile. Even Mr. Christmas has a glow about him. Not you."

The honesty knocked her off balance. The walls, peeling paint, faded stenciling, and sad exhibits felt like they were closing in on her. She leaned onto the countertop that housed the Santa figures and blew out a breath.

The teacher looked to Nathan, and then her. "Miss, are you okay? Nathan, what did you do?"

Nathan answered before she could catch her breath. "We're talking about why she hates Christmas and is unhappy to be here."

Uncle Nick glanced in her direction as the boy blurted his assessment, catching Holly wiping tears.

Kevin's jaw muscles tightened with each word Nathan uttered. He thought he'd be used to the boy's insights after years knowing his best friend's son, but Nathan still carried a shock value. He looked around for a tissue, but Mr. Christmas pulled out a box behind the counter and handed it to the petite woman who looked like she could collapse at any moment.

He cleared his throat, suddenly void of moisture. "Mr. Christmas, maybe we should leave. I apologize for the students."

The older man waved him off. "Nonsense. We need your help, everyone's help. Right, Holly?"

She dabbed her eyes with a shaky hand and nodded. "I'm sorry, it's me. It's my first time back here since I left ten years ago. There's a lot of memories."

Nathan jumped in. "Miserable ones."

Kevin placed a firm hand on the boy's shoulder. "Please don't say another word."

The rest of the class used the distraction to shuffle away and down toward the stairway. The visit was getting completely out of control. "I need everyone to find a partner and stay here."

The kids paired off and found their way around him.

"Mr. Christmas—"

Another wave of the hand. "Call me Uncle Nick. All of you." The man's smile was as warm as a plate of cookies fresh out of the oven.

The woman with soft curls and wide green eyes offered a similar grin. "I'm Miss Holly. Uncle Nick needs to show us around so we know what needs to be done to make Christmas Mansion the place to visit in Geneseo Valley all year around."

Uncle Nick took his niece's cue and started down the hall toward the stairs. "I'll warn you, things are a bit disorganized up there. It's where my brother had all his ideas, but not a lot was ready to be on display."

Kevin gripped the wobbly railing as shoes stomped up the steps. He thought of different skills he could teach the class like measurements, cutting, painting, and maybe if they responded well, the kids might be able to drill and hammer. Kevin reached the top and the kids parted like the Red Sea as Kevin entered the three rooms that were transformed to one room with no dividers.

There were plastic soldiers, angels, wooden fences, Styrofoam snowflakes, and strands upon strands of Christmas bulbs that looked at least twenty years old. Every corner and spot on the floor was covered with random holiday-themed objects.

Holly tried to move further into the room, but layers of tulle blocked her path. "Oh, Dad. Did you finish anything here?"

One of the students, Allie, leaned in. "Mr. Holt, who is she talking to?"

"I think she's kind of praying."

She nodded. "Yeah, if I owned this mess, I'd pray too. Do we really have to make this our community project?"

All heads turned toward him.

Chapter Three

Hours after the students left the Christmas mansion, Holly traipsed around upstairs, trying to process the chaos around her. Her father always took pride in the mansion's excellent condition. The place looked more like a hoarder's showcase. She picked up a fractured nativity figurine and examined it. *So much brokenness.*

Holly heard footsteps and a drawn-out sigh as she turned toward the door. Uncle Nick shook his head. "I tried to keep up, but he had so much stuff, so many ideas."

"And so little time. I didn't realize it had been so long since I'd visited. The last time I was here, the mansion hummed along with retro exhibits. The kids clambered to meet with Santa Chris." Holly closed her eyes and recalled the wonder of her school friends sharing their dreams with her dad, clad in a pristine Santa suit. The pain of him not finding time for her, yet being there for everyone else, re-opened her wound.

Her uncle shuffled closer, sidestepping boxes of ornaments. "Holly, your father loved you so much. He had perfect words as Santa, but I know Chris struggled when it came to telling you his feelings. He hoped you would love this place as much as he did. His prayer was you'd come back."

She sucked in the stale air. "I can't believe the boy from the tour told everyone I hate Christmas."

He chuckled. "Was he right?"

Holly shifted her weight as she looked for an escape. "When I asked him why he said that, his response was I didn't have a glow. When it comes to Christmas, I don't. I never did. It was our life. But maybe it was this place I hated." She sighed and stretched. "Now, I need to bring it back to life."

Quiet filled the room. Holly still planned her exit strategy so she wouldn't trip. Grief pounded through her like an unrelenting migraine. So many regrets.

Uncle Nick broke the silence. “Do you have an idea?”

She glanced at her scraps of scribbled notes as she scanned the room. “Thoughts. Nothing concrete.”

“Any of those involve Mr. Holt from this morning?”

Holly grinned at the thought of his kind smile and handsome face with a couple days’ beard growth. “With the energy those kids have, they will be perfect to haul this room out. I don’t know much about what this place needs, except updating.”

Another laugh. “You didn’t answer my question.”

She rolled her eyes. He was as discerning as Nathan was earlier. “I know.”

Kevin tossed his jacket on the couch and fell onto the plump pillows in a tired heap. Nathan trailed behind, mimicking his teacher’s actions by doing the same with the recliner.

Nathan’s head popped up from the cushion. “You exhausted? I’m beat.”

Kevin closed his eyes, wishing Jonah, his best friend since elementary school, would walk through the doors and deal with his son. “Nathan, why was Miss Holly in tears today? Did you say something that might have hurt her feelings? Remember our talk about sharing kind words?”

Nathan nodded. “I was nice, Kevin. Promise. I was also honest.”

Ugh. That would explain it. Nathan’s transparency produced a lot of tears. Kevin opened his eyes and sat up. “I love that you tell the truth, Bud. I do. But you have to watch how you say things, and when. Does that make sense?”

Before Nathan could respond, the garage door opened and the boy was off to meet his dad. Kevin stood and looked up. “Lord, running out of strength here.”

A couple of minutes later, Jonah Welling walked into the living room, Nathan's heels at his father's ankles. Nathan was talking at hummingbird speed about the Christmas Mansion. "I promise, we didn't break anything this time. We go back next week. I think we could work there for ten years and it still wouldn't be done."

Kevin caught Jonah's attempt to hide a laugh. "Nathan, your mom loved Christmas Mansion. She used to get so excited to see Santa Chris when she was a little girl. She even worked there when we were at college."

Nathan's eyes widened as his dad mentioned Lily. "I'm going to do a good job there. For Mom."

Kevin's throat constricted as Jonah tussled Nathan's hair. "Bud, she'd love that."

Once they threw together a salad and grilled hamburgers for dinner, Nathan settled in his room to tackle homework. Jonah turned on the television and reached in the couch cushion before pulling out the remote. "So, Kev, how was the Christmas Mansion? Can the kids make a difference?"

Kevin let out a low whistle. "Nathan wasn't exaggerating. The man who ran it and played Santa passed away. His brother has been trying to keep the place going, but it's overwhelming. Holly Christmas is the daughter, she apparently is back to help."

Jonah looked over. "Lily used to talk about Holly. They grew up together. Holly was even offered a full scholarship to Geneseo like Lily, but she rejected it. Holly left Geneseo Valley right after high school."

Kevin nodded. "Holly seemed shocked at what the place looked like. She also appeared sad, something Nathan wasted no time in sharing with her."

Jonah sighed. "I'm so glad you're his teacher. Between Nathan's diagnosis journey we were on with the doctors before Lily got sick, and all the emotions with her gone, few would understand all he's going through. I know all your students are struggling in some way."

"They are, but they have so much to contribute. Not only to their education, but to their community. I've been wracking my brain all afternoon trying to think of ways we can use our skills to help Holly."

Jonah chuckled. "You mean the mansion?"

Kevin shot a pillow at his friend. "Same thing, Holly, mansion."

Jonah caught the pillow and played with it. "Sure it is. How about involving the college? The university and Christmas Mansion are the anchors of Geneseo Valley. I know back in the day I took a class where I had to create a publicity plan for a struggling business. It's free help, and the students need the experience."

Kevin glanced up. "That's perfect. I'm going to call Holly first thing tomorrow. Once we have a plan in place, I'm sure we could involve a sorority and fraternity to assist my class. You know how that saying goes, 'Many hands make light work.'"

Jonah threw the pillow back at Kevin like it was a frisbee. "I know another saying. Wanna hear it?"

Kevin shrugged, treating the cushion as if it were a baseball, tossing it back to Jonah. "Sure, go ahead."

Jonah busted out in song as he caught the pillow and held it. "Kevin and Holly sitting in a tree. K-i-s-s-i-n-g."

Before Kevin could respond, Nathan slid in on the wooden floors with his worn socks, facing Jonah. "Dad, what are you singing? Can I sing it, too?"

Chapter Four

Holly beat Uncle Nick to the mansion the next morning, determined to get a head start on organizing the gift shop. Once she turned all the lights on and made a pot of coffee, she took her iPad out of her briefcase and pulled up the gift shop blueprints she created.

The app helped her plan out the space, and she sipped her hot beverage as she perused the plans. Her first goal was to take out the Christmas tree in the front window, clean the glass, and use the space for monthly displays. *Sounds easy, but I don't think that tree's been moved in years.*

Twenty minutes later, Holly rooted herself in the front corner, reaching out for the top of the now bare tree. The artificial needles tickled her nose as she jerked the six-foot pine toward her. The front door sleigh bells shook, signaling someone entering the lobby.

Uncle Nick's chuckle bounced off the cream walls. "Holly? Girl, what are you doing? That tree should be dismantled first."

She gently placed it back to its original position and backed up until she could see him shaking his head as he took off his jacket. "I tried, believe me. Everything's rusted together. And the tree feels so heavy. It isn't moving as easily as I thought."

He puttered toward her, pushing his glasses down his nose as he glanced around the area. "I see one problem."

Holly trailed behind him, wondering what she missed.

Uncle Nick reached around to the front of the tree and seemed to pull at it. He turned to face her, producing a spun glass decoration in his hand. "I don't think this is why the tree is heavy, but I can say I'm glad you didn't move it yet. You missed the crystal decorations that the Corning glassblowers made for us."

Holly felt a tightening in her temples. Those ornaments were exclusive, she remembered Dad raving about them the day they were delivered. She recalled also in the mail that day was her first college acceptance. "I need another cup of coffee. I can't believe I forgot to take those down. I can do it. You have other things to do, I'm sure." She grasped the clear glass with care.

"I can go upstairs and start clearing that out, but if we work together room by room, wouldn't that help?"

She shrugged. "I suppose. I thought if I could at least make the gift shop look presentable, I wouldn't feel so overwhelmed."

Uncle Nick shuffled to the storage closet off the gift shop and returned with padding and a plastic bin. "Here. Pack the ornaments, and I'll keep looking around to see why it's weighed down. I'm not much help, but I'm glad you're here. Your Ohio life was probably more exciting, but this is an answer to my prayer."

A stab of guilt pricked at her stomach. Holly's Ohio life had been intentionally far removed from family and their Christmas traditions. When her corporate marketing job disappeared and her colleagues didn't return her calls, she understood true loneliness for the first time. Sure, Dad threw his life into the Christmas Mansion, but while Holly was growing up, he was still at home every night for her. He provided for college. Bragged on her to friends at his church. By the time she realized how her adult choices shut her father out, he was gone.

Holly gingerly moved to the front, taking the glass pieces off and folding them in the padding. "I should have moved back earlier. Before Dad—"

Uncle Nick was next to her, spreading the branches. "He passed knowing you loved him very much. He's with Jesus and your mother now."

She nodded and focused on steadying her hand. "I was so angry with him when I moved away. I didn't try at all to make things right. Even as a teen I focused on how neglected I felt as a kid. It was so selfish."

Nick bent down to the base. "Your feelings were normal. You lost your mom and were grieving. Chris channeled his pain into this place, wanting to make families happy. He didn't see until after you left that the one family member not impressed by the mansion was his own daughter." He wiggled with the bottom. "Okay, mystery solved. He put coins in here. Forgot all about it."

Holly squinted as she tried to look at Nick's discovery. "To weigh it down?"

He straightened. "I don't think so. I remember closing with him one night and I watched him pour some coins into the second hole in the base. I asked him what was he doing and he explained that after a tour, he'd receive tips and he hid them in the tree. Once he filled the base, he donated to a charity."

Holly put her hands on her heart. "Oh, Daddy. What a kind soul." She returned to the front window. "Let me get the last of these ornaments so we can try to get the tree out of the base." She packed up the remaining three and put the bin aside before joining Uncle Nick.

He was on his knees, twisting the bottom of the tree, grunting. "You weren't kidding. This is rusted."

She wrapped her hands around the middle section, rotating back and forth, hoping the tree would give. The sleigh bells jingled again. "Just a sec, someone's at the door."

Before she could back up, a male voice greeted them. "Good morning. I meant to call, but I took a chance and thought I'd stop by. Can I help?"

Holly released her grip and turned, facing the handsome teacher she met the day before. *Time to wipe the cobwebs out of my hair.*

Kevin froze as soon as he locked eyes with Holly Christmas. He gulped as she stepped forward, black strands of hair near her eyes.

Holly extended her hand. "Hello, Mr. Holt, right? We're fighting with a stubborn tree. My dad left change in the base, and the tree appears rusted to it. You didn't come for that, though. What can I do for you?"

He tried to find his voice as he kept his focus on Holly. "Call me Kevin. I have a few minutes before I need to get to the school, so I can lend a hand with the tree, and I can tell you about an idea I have."

She tilted her head and raised her eyebrows. "Deal. I admit I'm curious."

The two walked toward Uncle Nick, kneeling while he shook the tree. Kevin stepped ahead and joined him on the floor. "Nick, let me do this. Take a break."

The older man smiled and took Holly's outstretched hand as he stood. "Perfect timing. My back isn't happy right now."

Holly gripped the middle as Kevin twisted. "Take a break, Uncle Nick. We've got this."

Before Nick was able to turn toward the counter, Kevin grunted and watched as the bottom gave way, rotating on the floor. The tree seemed to fall slow-motion to the other side, Holly letting go as it fell. "Look at that. You two are a dynamic duo!" The senior citizen chuckled.

Kevin rubbed his hands together. "You loosened it, Sir."

Holly wiped her palms on her jeans. "I'm glad it's done. If you're able to tip it to pour out the coins, that would be a great help."

He nodded and retrieved the plastic green circle. It took two hands to lift, but he carried it to the counter and poured the contents over the glass. Metallic smells and stale air penetrated the atmosphere. "Nice chunk of change."

Holly nodded. "I just learned Daddy kept tips in the base, then collected it for charity." Her eyes seemed to water, but she swiped at the corner of them before Kevin could know for sure.

"That's a great gesture." He glanced at his watch. "I hate to be in a rush, but I have a class at ten. I wanted to talk to you about an idea. My best friend and I got talking last night and he reminded me that the college has a public relations class that comes up with community projects. It's their job to create a marketing proposal to help the assigned business out."

Holly looked to Nick, who shrugged. "I never thought of that. Perhaps that group can come up with a great plan, and then your class can help execute it."

Kevin nodded. "That's what I thought. Would you like me to call the professor and set up something?"

Her eyes brightened. "Would you? That's a huge help."

He took out his phone and added a reminder. "Sure thing. So, what are you going to do with the tree?"

She snapped her fingers as she glanced around, then said, "I'd like to put it in the corner where we start the tour and decorate it throughout the year. There are artists who worked with Dad that created collections for all the seasons and holidays."

Uncle Nick scratched at his white mustache. "I can see it now. Easter eggs, shamrocks, flags, and pumpkins."

Holly smiled. "Don't forget the hearts. Lots of them for Valentine's Day."

Kevin grimaced as he pulled his keys out of his pocket. "No, anything but that."

She cocked her eyebrows once again. "What are you talking about?"

He sighed. "I hate Valentine's Day."

Chapter Five

A week after Kevin and his class arrived at the mansion to start cleaning the upstairs, Holly kept thinking about his Valentine's confession. What was the story behind those mesmerizing sapphire eyes? She was still entranced by the question when he entered the gift shop, followed by four young adults.

"Good morning, Holly! As promised, I have a group of Geneseo students who will be using The Christmas Mansion for their public relations project." He gestured to the tall, thin girl with long, curly, fire-engine red hair. "This is Rachel, then Jessica, Ian and Adam. Everyone, meet Holly Christmas."

Jessica glanced around at the dusty shelves and cobwebs in the gift shop and shrugged. "We have our work cut out for us."

Ian held out his hand. "Nice to meet you, Miss Christmas. I came here years ago as a little kid. I was always scared to sit on the mall Santa's lap, but never with Santa Chris. That was your dad, right?"

Holly nodded, a stab of nostalgia hitting her in the gut. "He had a way of calming kids. My Uncle Nick is also very sweet with the children. Did you want to meet in the video room? We have chairs set up as part of the tour."

With united, mumbled, "Sure," she led the way to the first stop after the gift shop sign-in. Kevin winked as she walked past him, his woodsy scent nearly buckled her at the knees.

Holly arranged the chairs in a circle. Kevin followed her, and within minutes, they were all sitting, gawking in her direction. "Does anyone know the history behind the mansion?"

Ian raised his hand, freckles dotting his elevated arm. "Your grandparents bought the land real cheap because it was near a railroad. Your grandfather loved the holiday because of his name and family traditions and decorated it for children. When your dad took over, he added exhibits upstairs and kept it open almost year-round."

Adam scratched at his patchy beard. "I Googled the name. Read that once your mom passed away, your dad kept everything going, but he refused to retire. A customer review said the tour became sad because the place was in dire need of an upgrade."

Holly's eyes sought a spot on the floor in an effort to find composure. She drew in a deep breath. "It's okay. Go on."

Adam cleared his throat. "Then your dad died, and his brother took over. The mansion has no social media presence. I couldn't find where you advertise. Although the gift shop looks nice, the exterior is faded and needs of a good landscaping team."

Holly opened her phone and started typing out notes. Social media was crucial. Why hadn't she thought of that? She glanced at the girls. "Rachel, Jessica, do you have anything to add?"

Rachel sat up, clutching her phone. "I jotted ideas as well. Social media was a question I had. You need to have a Facebook page, Instagram account, maybe even Pinterest."

Jessica coughed. "True, but it's a waste if people are aware of the place and come, only to learn it's full of stale air and old stuff our grandparents wouldn't even put on a tree."

Kevin leaned forward, facing her. "Jessica, part of public relations is presentation. Make sure you're promoting yourself in the most professional way possible."

The girl with trendy, round, black glasses rolled her eyes. "I'm speaking the truth. Miss Christmas needs to hear it. This place is a joke to the college kids, and any business you get is out of tradition and pity." She turned her attention from Kevin to Holly. "And I did some research as well. If this place means so much to you, where were you when it was falling apart?"

An hour later, after the students left, Kevin leaned up against the gift shop door. It wasn't a terrible meeting; in fact, they left with a plan in place to start a social media campaign and research ideas to bring the mansion up-to-date with tours and exhibits. He peeked over at Holly, who stood near the register, typing on her phone. He walked toward her. "You okay?"

Her sigh spoke volumes. "Jessica was brusque, but she nailed it. The place is falling apart and I could have stopped it. I should have stayed in town and went to college here. I never should have left him alone with this."

He placed his hand on her arm. "Holly, none of this is your fault. It's an aging establishment in a small, college town. I'm not sure if you've looked around the area, but there are a lot of empty storefronts on this street."

Holly turned toward him and put the phone down, glancing at his hand on her. He quickly pulled it away, the glass counter separating them. "You don't understand, Kevin. I love your enthusiasm, but before I left for college, Daddy begged me to reconsider. He said I could get an excellent education here, and I'd also be able to help him."

Kevin rested his arms on the counter, trying to find the right words as he gazed into her sad eyes. "I think every father wants their little girl to stay home."

She shook her head and looked away. "This was different. I took pleasure in moving away. I was only thinking of myself and the opportunities I had away from Geneseo Valley and the mansion."

It took complete focus not to touch her, or place his hand on hers. "I was the same, Holly. I left my hometown to attend college here. I didn't think about my parents missing me at all. It's normal."

Her laugh sounded more like a strangled cry. "It's not the same. He begged me to stay and I snickered in his face with my reply. I'm sure I broke his heart that day."

Kevin glanced around to find her a tissue. "You're being too hard on yourself. I'm sure you remember it worse than it really was."

Her lush green-eyes pierced his heart. “Kevin. I told him I’d never stay here because—I hate Christmas.”

Chapter Six

Holly allowed herself an extra hour of sleep Sunday morning, but rose with determination. After her homemade bulletproof coffee for breakfast, she opened her laptop and retrieved all her notes from the cloud.

While reading over her to-do list for Kevin's students, she stopped half-way. *Kevin.* For someone she recently met, he occupied a lot of her thoughts. After her confession about what she said to her father, Kevin didn't judge her. He was the first person besides Uncle Nick she'd ever shared that moment with. Holly smiled just reading his name. *Girl, you've got it bad.*

Her phone ringing several times pulled her back to the kitchen island workspace. She snatched it from her pocket and glanced at the screen and smiled. "Good morning, Uncle Nick."

"Holly, I'm back from church and wanted to invite you to brunch. My treat."

Her coffee mug emptied, but the creamy drink left her stomach growling in protest. "Sounds good. Tell me where, and I'll meet you there."

Thirty minutes later, Holly pulled into the Denny's lot next to Uncle Nick's compact car. He loved his diners, just like her father had. She walked in and spotted her favorite senior citizen across the room in a corner booth. She observed the empty tables as she strolled by. "Hey, apparently the college group that usually comes here is still sleeping." Holly tossed her purse inside the booth and scooted in next to it.

He looked up from the menu and smiled, wrinkles creasing near his eyes. "Perhaps they're at church."

Holly shot him a grimace, but his menu was upright and he appeared engrossed in reading it. Between her confession to Kevin and Nick's barb, guilt seemed to be the special of the week. "Once I get settled, I'll look for a church home."

His expression didn't change. "You used to go to church all the time when you were growing up."

The waitress stopped to pour water and take their order before Holly could reply. "I went because my parents did. After mom passed, we went because it was her last request."

He took a sip from his glass. "Holly, you're carrying a heavy load of grief. I don't have all the answers to make you happy, but I know Jesus wants to take your burdens. He can handle everything."

Holly waved the thought off. "I need time. I've had trouble making sense of a loving Father taking my mother away."

Uncle Nick flinched. "I see. I don't mean to upset you. I love you as if you were my daughter."

She grimaced, then softened. "I'm sorry, I know you mean well. I promise, once I settle in, I will find a church. Now, do you want to hear the latest mansion plans?"

Before Nick could reply, he looked up and smiled. Holly turned and saw Kevin with Nathan, another man Kevin's age, and a young woman that looked to be in her early twenties. Holly's heartbeat accelerated at the sight of the teacher wearing a ski vest to match his blue eyes. The waitress greeted the group and gestured them to follow her. As they obeyed, Kevin put his arm on the woman's shoulder, sending Holly's heart to a shallow grave.

Kevin allowed Jonah's sister Natalie to slide inside the vinyl half-circle booth before he sat on the end across from Nathan. He glanced around the room and noticed Nick Christmas smiling as the waitress placed a plate of steaming food in front of him. *Is that Holly?* "Hey, Jonah, if the waitress comes for my order, I'll take a plain hamburger with fries. Coke. I'm going to say hello to Nick Christmas."

Nathan's head turned as Kevin stood. "Can I go? I see Miss Holly."

Jonah placed a protective hand on his son's arm. "How 'bout we let Kevin visit with them this time, okay?"

Kevin wiped his hands on his jeans as he closed in on the Christmas booth. Nick grinned as Kevin approached, his hand outstretched. "Uncle Nick, hello." They greeted each other as Holly sat, eyeing them, her shamrock-colored eyes captivating Kevin's attention.

"What brings you out this fall afternoon, son?"

Kevin wiped the back of his neck and tried to casually glance in Holly's direction before answering Nick. "Church's over and thought we'd go to lunch."

The older man's eyebrows raised when church was mentioned. "Is that right? Would you like to join us?"

It was a reflex to keep looking at Holly in hopes she wouldn't notice. "I wish I could, but I think my friends would be upset. Holly, Nathan wanted to come over to say hello. I think he might have a little crush on you."

She chuckled and turned to the booth, where Nathan and the adults were staring in her direction. "I'll make sure to say hello before I leave."

Kevin's throat went dry. He needed water, fast. "Great. I'll let you both eat. Good to see you."

Uncle Nick opened his napkin and placed it on his lap. "Looking forward to seeing you at the mansion. Holly says you have some great ideas."

Kevin nodded. "Yes, between my students and the Geneseo public relations class, I think there's a great plan in motion. Have a good lunch." He retreated before his voice cracked. What was it about that shiny, black hair and mint-colored eyes that made him lose all composure?

Concentrating on putting one foot in front of the other as he made his way back to his booth, he noticed his best friend since grade school was grinning like a Cheshire cat.

"Do Natalie and I get to meet the famous Holly Christmas? She's all you and Nathan talk about." Jonah noted.

Kevin guzzled from his water glass before replying. "She said she'll say goodbye on her way out. You two need to behave. You two are like my own siblings, but don't you dare embarrass me. Holly's been through a lot."

Natalie's eyes widened and she put her hand on her heart. "Did you hear that, Jonah? Kevin thinks we'll do something to mortify him."

Nathan put his spoon in his glass and tried to fish for a piece of ice. "What's mortify?"

Jonah leaned toward his son. "Kevin thinks we're going to tease him when Miss Holly comes to say hello. We wouldn't, though. We don't want him to get mad at us and move out, do we?" The tween kept angling for a piece of ice. "No way. He makes great grilled cheese sandwiches. Way better than Aunt Natalie when she visits."

The adults exchanged looks and stifled a laugh. Nathan and his priorities.

Kevin was half way through his French fries when Holly strolled over to their booth as Uncle Nick paid the bill. She focused on Nathan as she gave a big smile. "Hello, Nathan. Did you order something good?"

He looked at his cheeseburger, and then Holly, his nose wrinkled. "I guess. Isn't food supposed to be good at a restaurant?"

Kevin stood. "Holly, I'd like to introduce you to my second family. This is Jonah, Nathan's father, and Natalie, Jonah's kid sister. She's in town for the weekend making sure we haven't completely trashed the house and that Nathan gets vegetables. Guys, this is Holly Christmas."

The siblings grinned and said hello.

Nathan picked at his bun. "Miss Holly lets me untangle lights so we can test them."

Holly chuckled. "You do a great job, too. I'm very happy you and your classmates are coming out to help me and Uncle Nick."

Natalie cleared her throat. "What kinds of things do you have the kids doing?"

"I have a group of college students working on a plan to make the community more aware of the mansion. They also have ideas to update the tour. Kevin's class has been cleaning out the upstairs. I'm grateful for all the help." She shot a look toward Kevin, and the two locked eyes.

Jonah broke their gaze. "My wife used to work at the mansion. She loved it."

Nathan shredded the bread between his thumb and index finger. "My mom died."

Holly moved closer to the table. "I'm so sorry, sweetie. My mom is gone, too."

Jonah blew out a long breath. "Kevin told us that your parents have both passed. I'm sorry for your losses."

She bit her lip and looked over to the register. Nick was near the door. "Thank you. Uncle Nick and I have each other, and the mansion. Speaking of, I need to go. I'll see you this week, Nathan. Goodbye, Kevin. Nice to meet you, Jonah and Natalie."

Nathan's voice rose as the room suddenly quieted. "Maybe you can marry Kevin and you won't be so lonely."

Chapter Seven

Kevin's heartbeat still rocketed as Jonah drove home. He craned his neck and found Nathan in the backseat humming a tune Kevin didn't recognize. *Nathan was completely innocent when he said such an embarrassing thing to Holly. Still…*

Jonah glanced toward the passenger seat. "You okay over there?"

Kevin stared at the Main Street foliage, a collage of oranges and yellow leaves scattered on the sidewalk. "Did Holly's face turn fire engine-red when Nathan made that remark?"

Jonah grinned. "It was more like cherry tomato. You were the fire truck."

Kevin sighed. "She's worked with the class a couple times now. She understands their quirks, right?"

Jonah turned off Main Street and made his way to the residential area outside the college town. "My friend, you've got it bad. Holly seems like an understanding woman. I wouldn't worry about it. Unless—"

Kevin glanced over. "What do you mean, 'unless?'"

Jonah shrugged. "You could use the situation as a reason to contact her. Call her, visit the mansion before your next time with the students. Do something with this crush you have."

Kevin slowly nodded. "I mean, if I touch base with her, it's out of concern. I don't want there to be any uncomfortable feelings. I'm not saying I have an infatuation with Holly Christmas."

Jonah pushed the garage door opener and pulled the vehicle in. "You've done nothing but talk about her since your first meeting. I watched you steal glances toward her booth the entire time we were at the restaurant. You had a dopey grin when she said hello to us." He turned toward Kevin, his mood sober. "Kevin, if you like her, and I believe you do, don't waste a moment. You aren't promised tomorrow."

The ignition off, Nathan scrambled out of the car and raced up the steps to the mud room. Kevin kept his hand on the door handle, but didn't try to leave. "I know our losses aren't the same. I'm a jerk for even sharing this. But I don't know if I can ever recover from Mallory."

Jonah exited the car and jammed the keys in his pocket. He strolled around to the passenger side and opened Kevin's door. "I understand where you're coming from, a deep hurt. My experience is a profound loss. It *is* different. My wife's in heaven and I don't know how I could ever marry again. Mallory broke your trust. All women aren't like her. Dude, you should contact Holly."

Kevin grinned and joined Jonah. "I know you invited me to live here to lend a hand with Nathan, but your friendship saved me during a critical time."

Jonah raised his eyebrows as he kicked his shoes off. "God knew what He was doing. I was swimming in grief and clueless on how to raise a son without Lily. She understood his delays and medical journey. Your coming here was an answer to prayer for all of us."

"You're right about all women not being like Mallory. Lily was truly a gem. You two were the cliched perfect couple."

Jonah swiped the corner of his eye as they entered the kitchen. "Not perfect, but blessed. I don't think your story is finished. Call Holly."

Holly unwrapped a chocolate mint and opened the proposals the college students pitched for the mansion. She was half-way through Rachel's bullet points on having a Facebook business page when her phone buzzed. She peeked at the screen. It was a local number, but she wasn't familiar with the identity. *It could be*

mansion related. She swallowed the candy and pressed 'Talk.' "Hello? This is Holly Christmas."

A male voice that sounded strangely hesitant struggled. "Hello? Hey, Holly, it's um, Kevin. Holt. The teacher?"

Holly beamed at the sound of Kevin's name and abandoned her work for the soft couch, where she curled up. "Of course. Is everything okay?"

A quick cough prefaced his reply. "That's why I'm calling. I wanted to make sure Nathan didn't offend you with what he said earlier. He means well, but as you've probably figured out, he lacks a filter at times."

She giggled, the boy's comments about her hating Christmas, his getting kicked out of a grocery store for breaking a pickle jar, and suggesting she marry Kevin all raced to her mind. "Nathan's a delight. I'm not upset at all. He's brought a smile more than once, and that's been helpful."

His tone evened out. "Great. I'm relieved. He's a good kid. All Nathan talks about lately is the mansion."

Holly cradled her knees to her chest as she pictured Kevin managing the students so they would stay on task for her. "I'm looking at the Geneseo proposals now. I hope to discover a plan that will utilize your students more than we do now. I enjoy having them help out."

"It builds their self-esteem and skills, so it's a win-win. Do you have a lot of reading to do? If it isn't too late, we could meet over coffee and I could look at them with you."

Chills danced through her spine as she straightened and stood. "Are you sure? There's a stack of papers. It would go faster if I had someone working with me."

"Absolutely. Jonah's been raving about this new coffee shop in Livingston. Do you want to meet there? It's about fifteen minutes away."

Holly recalled hearing about the family run business called Papa Bear's. "I can be there in a half hour." Her light laughter filled the room. "Don't forget your glasses."

"Oh, you've seen those? I'm pretty vain about them, but I usually wear them nights to give my contacts a rest." He chuckled. "Anyway, I'll see you soon."

Holly ended the call and waltzed her way from the living room to her dresser to find something other than a sweatshirt to wear. It probably wasn't a date, but she didn't want Kevin to look at her and decide she was in as sad shape as the mansion. *Okay, girl, you can do this. Put on a nice sweater and spray some perfume.* Holly realized she was still dancing through the hallways as she got ready, grabbing her purse and taking the keys as she started to close the door. Before she locked up, she sighed and jogged back to the table where the proposals sat, nearly forgotten.

Thirty minutes later, she pushed on the heavy wooden door and instantly inhaled a dark roast aroma mixed with a wood fire. She looked across the room and spotted Kevin near a stone fireplace, orange flames restrained by a decorative screen. He stood and waved, gesturing for her to join him.

Holly chose an oversized leather chair across from Kevin and the heat. "This place is beautiful. It has such rustic charm. I love the wood."

He nodded. "It really is beautifully constructed. I ordered a cup of regular coffee, boring, I know. I wasn't sure what you would want, but I'm happy to order for you."

She turned and noticed the walnut counter with a barista, who like many other employees in the area, most likely attended SUNY Geneseo. Above the young woman was a chalkboard menu that stretched across the wall. "Wow, so many choices. I can order, thank you, though. I'll be back in a few."

Kevin nodded as she stood and strolled over to the gorgeous counter area. Holly perused the professional chalk artwork that was the menu. After deciding on a caramel macchiato, she returned with a ceramic mug filled with steamy goodness.

He pointed to the stack of papers under her elbow. "How far did you get? Anything good in there?"

Holly lifted a black folder. "Ian. Take a look before I say more."

Their fingers grazed as Kevin retrieved the proposal from her. Holly shivered and reached for more papers, hoping he didn't notice.

After a few minutes of shuffling pages, Kevin looked up, his face as lit up as the mansion in December. "Holly, this is genius. Winning grant money to win bids for Christmas props from movies and NYC store window displays? Transforming the mansion to an accessible tour full of re-creating cinematic moments we cherish? Walking through rooms that are like Christmas on steroids? It takes The Christmas Mansion from a cute novelty to visit to a must-see tourist stop."

Holly's hands shook. *Is this the electricity between Kevin and me, or the excitement we share from Ian's idea?* "So, I'm not crazy to love this plan?"

He chuckled. "If you are, then I'm right there with you. We can get the community involved. Donations. Grants. Youth groups could help my class clean out and make space. The college kids could work with honor society students from high school to search for online auctions and make bids."

Holly blinked and tears rolled down her cheeks. "Kevin, will you work with me and Uncle Nick on the logistics? Be part of the executive team?"

Kevin closed the folder and slid it back to her. He kept his hand on top as he grinned. "I only have one question before I say yes."

Her eyes widened and she felt a lump form in her throat. What would he possibly want? "Okay. You're making me nervous."

"It's a quick question, and I promise, I'll help either way."

She narrowed her gaze and folded her arms against her chest. "I'm listening."

"Do you consider tonight a date?"

Chapter Eight

Kevin stole another glance at Holly as she sorted through boxes of colorful foam shapes her father kept in storage. Even days after their coffee "gathering," the definition she gave instead of a date, he couldn't stop thinking about her. She possessed amazing business sense, and her passion for the mansion was obvious. Then that shy smile and those bright eyes that twinkled every time she giggled.

"Nathan, I need you and Rory to look through these boxes in the corner. If they are foam shapes, place them in the black garbage bags." She stood for a moment to ensure they understood the assignment. Rory tossed the plastic trash containers over to Nathan, while Nathan used the decorations as frisbees aimed at Rory. Holly shook her head and smiled as she looked for the next task.

The boys left the doorway and joined Holly in the back of the storage room. Kevin ran his hand through his hair and moved toward them. "Can I help?"

Holly turned as he crept closer, nearly smacking into his chest. "I think the boys can manage. Do you want to find my laptop downstairs and research grants and contact the Chamber of Commerce?"

His shoulders sunk as he realized his enthusiasm took him further from Holly, not closer. "Sure. Anything else?"

She glanced at her watch. "No, that's probably all the time we'll have before you have to leave."

Her words were clipped and almost dismissive, sending Kevin's stomach to wavy nausea.

Like a child being sent to the time-out chair, Kevin descended the stairs to find the laptop. Uncle Nick was in the gift shop, ringing out a family buying the glass bulbs Holly showcased in the front window. Kevin peeked behind the counter and spotted the computer. Once the customers left, Kevin joined him and retrieved the device.

The older man patted Kevin on the back. "What brings you downstairs?"

He shrugged. "Helping Holly find grants."

Nick chuckled. "You sound like you're about to get a root canal. Not your favorite job?"

"I guess not. Thought maybe the boys could use my assistance."

The elder scratched his chin. "That's too bad. Was that Holly's decision?"

Kevin swallowed hard. "Yes, sir."

Nick turned and scooted over to the wooden cabinet that stored inventory. He pulled out a box of ornaments and held them, facing Kevin. "Holly's scared. There's been a lot of loss in her life, and she's put up some walls to protect herself."

Kevin booted up the laptop and focused on the screen.

Nick balanced the box and strolled over to the front window ceiling hooks, replacing the ornaments. With an empty box, he returned to the counter. "Don't give up. My niece is worth fighting for."

Kevin looked up and met the man's kind smile. "Thank you. I really needed the encouragement. You know, the laptop is mobile. If you don't need me, I could just take this upstairs to do my work."

Nick's laugh sounded like Santa's. "You do that. Have fun."

Holly waded through the layers of boxes that dominated the middle of the room. The rest of the class seemed content opening various containers as if it were Christmas.

Isaac waved greenery like a lasso. "Miss Holly! Why are there berries in here?"

She opened a lid and bit her lip to avoid a sneeze. She glanced at the boy. “That’s mistletoe. If that all that’s in there?”

He took that as an invitation to dive further and produce plastic strands.

Nathan looked over and smirked. “That’s the kissing decoration. We used to have one.”

That was enough to disrupt Rory’s work flow, so he left Nathan and sidled over to Isaac. “Why’s there so much of it? Was there a kissing booth?”

The kids all stopped their work and started to laugh. Holly took a deep breath. They were so innocent, but there was a bit of work to do. “I don’t know. My dad probably had an idea to use it as part of a room. Let me peek at it.” She stood and navigated through the clutter. The garland looked like it came from the 1970’s. Musty smell. Waxy texture. She scrunched her nose. “I think this stuff is past its prime. You can toss it.”

Isaac, working through comprehension issues, cocked his head as he stared at Holly. “Toss it? To you?”

Before she could answer, Kevin stepped through the doorway. “How about to me?”

Holly’s heartbeat could qualify for NASCAR. “What are you doing?”

The boys grabbed the leafy mistletoe and held it over their heads, ready to throw it to their teacher. Kevin jogged over to them, laptop at his side, and took the old decorations with his free hand. “My grandma used to twist this on her staircase.”

Holly tapped her foot. “I thought you were downstairs.”

He let the garland fall and strolled over to a table with only a few knickknacks on it. He placed the laptop on it and returned to the boys. “Now I’m upstairs. The Wi-Fi works anywhere. I thought I’d join everyone here.”

Holly managed a tight smile, the situation felt out of control. “Of course. Well, find a place if you can.”

Kevin nodded, but picked up a strand. "This brings back a lot of memories. My grandpa used to call grandma to the bottom of the staircase and kiss her, always pointing to the cheesy mistletoe décor."

Holly stood still, wondering if her parents ever did the same. She gazed at Kevin, only to lock eyes with him, so she cleared her throat and directed her attention toward Nathan. His lips puffed out and he was exhausting himself trying to slam the foam shapes into the garbage. "You okay, Nathan?"

The boy stopped and slowly looked around the room, ending his pout with Kevin. "This place stinks." He kicked at the garbage bag and stomped over to the mistletoe, attacking it with waving arms and unintelligible cries.

Holly's eyes widened and she ran towards him, but Kevin held his arm out and prevented her from getting near. She stepped back and watched the others. They didn't move, except for Rory, who started to twitch.

Kevin put his arms around Nathan in a bear hug and held tight, whispering to him. Holly's eyes darted between them and the others. She reached into her pocket and grasped her phone, ready to pull it out and call for help if needed.

After a couple minutes, Nathan stopped struggling and just cried. Kevin kept his arm around him and they started to walk through the door. He turned toward Holly. "Do you mind watching them for a couple minutes? We'll be back to get everyone for the van."

She nodded. "Is he okay?"

Kevin bowed his head. "He misses his mom."

Holly gasped and quickly made her way to them, her gaze seeking Kevin's permission to come closer and engage with Nathan. Kevin nodded, letting go of him.

"Nathan, would it be okay if I talked to you?"

He turned around, his eyes bloodshot. His hands still balled in fists. She reached for them and touched the top of his knuckles. She felt his grip loosen. "Are you going to kick me out?"

Holly shook her head and positioned herself so she was looking not only into his teddy bear eyes, but into his hurting soul. She lost sight of everything and everyone except the tween trying to avoid her gaze. "I'm not. I understand you have to leave soon, but my mom is gone, too. Are you aware there's times a smell or a memory hits me and it overwhelms me?"

He examined her with arched eyebrows. "How does it overwhelm you?"

"It depends, and I don't always know until the feelings hit. Sometimes I'm so mad. I miss her. She wasn't at my graduation or college events. There are so many times I want her advice and—I'm alone."

Nathan exhaled a shaky breath. "My dad can't cook like mom did. Kevin tries to pray like she used to, but it isn't the same. No one hugs even close to how she used to." He started to cry, and fell into her arms. Holly glanced at Kevin, who gestured for her to continue. She held the boy, stroking his hair as she remembered her mom doing for her.

Ten minutes later, Nathan's tears ceased and he used a wet paper towel to clean up his face. Holly accompanied them out, saying goodbye to each student as they boarded the van.

Kevin finished the head count and faced her. "Holly, thank you. That was amazing what you did for Nathan. You took a tense situation and diffused it. He trusts you."

She looked above her to the left, where Nathan sat, grinning. His positive mood helped her smile back at Kevin. "I can relate to his pain. We have a plan to work through it together, if that's okay."

Kevin raised an eyebrow. "Sure thing. Honestly, it will be good for both of you. I have to get back to school, but I'd love to hear more."

Holly bit her lip before tumbling her words. "Would you like to have coffee again? If you want, it could be a date."

Chapter Nine

Holly tugged at her long, mauve sweater dress as she glanced in the office mirror. Kevin was due to pick her up for their date any minute. She heard a chuckle and found Uncle Nick behind her. "What's so funny?"

"You're spending so much time getting ready. That boy wouldn't care if you greeted him wearing a sack." He shuffled closer and rested his hand on her shoulder.

She turned and opened her arms for his hug. "I disagree. Kevin has been wonderful with all the mansion improvements, but I don't think he's going to book a chapel tonight."

Nick's eyes twinkled. "Perhaps not this evening, but I think I hear wedding bells."

Holly studied him for a moment, as his smirk grew into laughter. She gave him a swat on the arm before walking up front. "Good thing I love you." She called out, reaching the counter.

"Say that again?" A male voice from the candy cane corner sent Holly's panic into overdrive.

Holly took another step into the gift shop and realized Kevin had let himself in while she and Uncle Nick were in the office. *Oh, no. He thinks I just declared my love for him.* Her knees locked as soon as she saw him in the navy cable knit sweater and black jeans. He swiped at a black curl in the middle of his forehead. She took a deep breath, let it out, and smiled. "Kevin, I didn't hear you. I was in the back with Uncle Nick. He was picking on me and I let him know it's a good thing I love him. Just joking around."

Kevin nodded and grinned. He walked toward her and thrust his hands out, a bouquet of pink carnations in wrinkled cellophane. "Uncle Nick's easy to love. These flowers are for you. I didn't think about a vase. I hope you have one here."

Holly reached for them, but instead, placed her hand on top of his. One look in those turquoise eyes, and she was slow to move yet again. As their hands lingered, Holly cleared her throat. "I have one, so no worries. Let me take care of these. They're gorgeous. Thank you."

Kevin stuffed his hands in his front pockets, a kind smile warming her from head to toe. "Don't rush. We have all evening."

Holly tripped as she returned to the office. Uncle Nick spotted the flowers and started to chuckle once again. "There are no wedding bells, Uncle Nick."

He pursed his lips and nodded. "Of course not."

Kevin tried not to stare as Holly returned from the back with the carnations in a tall, crystal vase. Her long black hair was clipped back in a ponytail, and he realized for the first time she had a sprinkle of freckles across her cheeks. He fidgeted with his sleeve and cleared his throat. "Beautiful vase."

Holly looked down at the floor before meeting his gaze. "It's from my mom's funeral. I have a few, but this one's my favorite."

Nice going, Kev. Way to make her sad on your date. "I didn't mean to bring up an unhappy memory."

Holly placed the flowers on the counter next to the cash register and then reached out and touched his arm. "No, it's fine. Although I have a lot of keepsakes from funerals, they aren't depressing to me. Anymore." She lifted her hand and retrieved her purse. "C'mon, let's go. I'm hungry. No more serious talk. "

He followed her lead by nodding and opening the front door for her, the clicking of Holly's heels matching the beating of his heart.

Twenty minutes later, Kevin pulled into Tarantelli's in Mount Morris. The restaurant was beloved by the locals for the matriarch's fresh garlic bread, and the patriarch's secret recipe for spaghetti sauce. Kevin's stomach growl echoed throughout the car as he parked.

Holly faced him. "Uncle Nick thinks Mr. and Mrs. Tarantelli somehow have a vent that pumps out the sauce fragrance throughout the village."

Kevin chuckled. "Let me open the door for you and see if you smell anything."

Once they were both out of the car, Holly inhaled deeply as if she were in the middle of a yoga class. "I think Uncle Nick might be onto something."

"You smell sauce?"

She nodded as he tenderly placed his hand on her back as they strolled to the restaurant front doors. "Not only that, but it gave me an idea. I'd love to create a Christmas sense of smell throughout the mansion. Switch it up each day, maybe. Peppermint. Pine. Even a sugar cookie scent."

Kevin opened the door for her, drinking in her sweet floral perfume as she passed by. There was no way he was going to be able to focus on her words when he was so enchanted by her beauty and passion for the mansion.

Holly cleared her throat. "Did you hear what I said?"

Busted. "I'm sorry, I lost my train of thought when you walked by. Sounds cheesy, but it's true."

She gave him a sweeping glance before breaking into a grin. "Forgiven. I wondered if wax melts are the way to go. I know the owner of Aromahh Candles down the block from the mansion. Maybe she can give me a deal if I purchase in bulk."

Kevin helped Holly to her seat and stood for a moment. For a woman who used to hate Christmas, she was thinking of brilliant ideas to help families re-discover the magic of the Christmas Mansion. *And at the same time, I think I'm falling in love with her.*

Holly took a bite of her chicken parmesan and closed her eyes as she savored her meal. When she opened them, the first thing she saw was Kevin. His mouth curved up, and his focus appeared to be on her in a gaze that went straight to her soul. Holly narrowed her stare. "What?"

Kevin played with his wrinkled napkin. "I'm fascinated by all you're doing with the mansion. How well you interact with my students, especially Nathan. I've never met anyone like you, Holly Christmas."

She rolled her eyes and giggled. "You're too kind. I go to bed near tears every night because I'm so tired and worried that I'm letting my parents down. I want the mansion to succeed because they poured so much love into it, and into each other."

Her heartbeat quickened when he reached across the table and squeezed her hand. "Your hard work is going to pay off. I'm certain your parents would be so proud. I heard about you all over town, even in the grocery store. Everybody's talking about how the mansion's really shaping up with landscaping and paint."

Holly's shoulders relaxed and she sipped her ice water. "You've been a big reason why things are progressing well."

"I don't know about that, but I'll confess I go to bed every night exhausted. I thank God that none of the students broke anything in the gift shop that day." He winked and chuckled softly.

They ate in silence for a few moments as Holly reflected on the motley group of students with various special needs. She broke the quiet with her proclamation. "You're a dynamic teacher. Not everyone could keep a group of middle school aged kids together, much less create consistent work from them. Not to forget they have struggles they're working on. Their improvement is thanks to you."

Kevin dabbed his chin with his napkin and waved her off. "I guess we're each other's biggest fan. I love what you've accomplished, and you admire my career."

Holly shook her head and studied him. "Speaking of love…"

Kevin stiffened in his chair.

She folded her arms against her chest. "I'm curious. Why do you hate Valentine's Day?"

Chapter Ten

Kevin wondered if he swallowed a chicken bone. He spewed a hearty cough and reached for his glass of ice water before daring to glance at Holly. When he finally did, her wide eyes reminded him of the warm gulf waters in Mexico. He gulped and set the drink down. "Wow. I thought maybe you'd forget I said that."

She blinked several times, completely fixated on him.

"Holly, I think we have a great connection. Like you, I want this relationship to blossom between us. That can't happen without complete honesty, so it's important that you know about my past. My trust was broken through a failed engagement when I was a senior in college."

Her fork clanged against the plate and she rushed to grab it as the other customers turned toward them. "You were going to get married?" Holly's voice sounded an octave higher than normal.

He breathed in slowly and ran a hand through his hair. "Yep. It was a while ago. I met Mallory in college, right in Geneseo Valley. We started dating our junior year, and my plan was for us to marry on Valentine's Day of our senior year."

Holly reached for her sweet tea. "What happened?"

"It played out like a bad movie. Everyone warned me Mallory was immature. I almost lost my friendship with Jonah over it. Turns out, everyone, especially Jonah, was right. She left me at the altar. Gave a note to our pastor. Everyone was there. By graduation, she was already dating someone else. Maybe she had been before then. I was a complete fool." Regret tinged his voice.

Holly placed her hand over her mouth and shook her head. "Kevin, that's terrible. I don't care how immature she might have been, no one should wound another person like that. She should have said something before the wedding. Way before then." She bit at her bottom lip for a moment. "It's her loss."

He shrugged. "I know now our marriage never would have worked. It took a long time to work through the rejection. Still not a fan of Valentine's Day, but I'm sure God will help me."

She pushed at her lettuce like a bulldozer. "Good for you. I have that tree in the hallway where I plan to decorate through the seasons. I'd love for your students to help me without fear that you might get angry and throw my crafted hearts on the ground." She lifted her head, revealing a grin.

Kevin chuckled. The darkness of that time in his life dissipated as he drank in Holly's warm smile. "I promise not to ruin any Valentine plans at the mansion or throw your heart on the ground."

Holly froze, her fork mid-stab into a grape tomato. "You mean hearts, right? My decorations."

"I meant your heart, Holly. I promise not to intentionally hurt you." He reached for her hand and held it, an electrical charge surging between them. "But I won't destroy your crafts, either."

Holly blew out hot air as she waited for Kevin to open her car door. Their date had been full of laughs, good food, and a scary dose of flirtation and confession. Her heartbeat picked up pace as she looked ahead to her front door.

He took her hand and helped her out of the car. "This was great. I had a lot of fun, Holly."

She nodded, her gaze focused on the porch light above her door. "Me, too. I guess the next time I'll see you is Monday? I hope to have Nathan work with me in the downstairs sitting room. Our goal is to collect thousands of ornaments and hang them from the ceiling. He even has an idea to create a makeshift chimney for families to go through so they can feel like Santa." Her words spilled out faster and more breathless the closer she reached the steps.

His grip on her hand tightened as he cleared his throat. "Nathan has to be the most creative kid I've ever met. If anyone can pull it off, he can. You know, we could meet earlier. If you want, that is."

She ambled up the wooden stairs and released his hand so she could dig her key out of her purse. "What do you mean?"

He stayed on the bottom step while she remained on the top, two inches apart. "Come to church with me tomorrow."

All romantic feelings tied to the night deflated like a balloon. She turned toward the door and fumbled with the lock. "Oh. Maybe another time. Thanks for a great night. Bye." The door slammed with more force than she intended, and she leaned against it with closed eyes as she heard footsteps leave the porch. Only when tires crunched the pebbles in her driveway did she dare open her eyes and throw herself on the couch. *Good going, Holly. You had an amazing evening with a wonderful man and blew it. Is church that bad? Is it?*

Teen memories re-surfaced with the surge of a tidal wave during a tsunami. Her mom's funeral and the ladies of the church hugging her, musky perfume that made her want to vomit. The Sundays she'd heard many of the same women whispering about her, calling her a "poor dear" or "that sad child." It didn't take long before the whispers became accusations. Why wasn't her father in church? How dare he create a career that profits from the birth of Christ? The final blow was when Holly volunteered to help at a banquet uniting women and girls over dinner and a fashion show. The coordinator, Mrs. Sallie Wong, cocked her head to the side and sighed. "Oh, dear, that's so nice of you. Perhaps you didn't know, we're having it Mother's Day weekend. We're not just kicking off a mentoring ministry, but celebrating mothers and daughters. I don't think that would work for you, do you?"

Ten years later, the anger still ran through her like lava. Kevin was an amazing first date. But if church attendance was a priority for him, Holly had no interest in pursuing a second.

Chapter Eleven

Kevin kept his hand on the mud room coat hook and stood still. Sure, he knew he wasn't Upstate New York's most eligible bachelor, but still. What made Holly slam the door in his face? He couldn't shake the panic in her eyes and the sound of the door as it shut, Holly firmly behind it. As he trudged toward the living room, the light from the television screen brought him back to reality.

Jonah greeted him with a smile and a bowl of potato chips. "How did it go?"

Kevin hitched his eyebrow and a sarcastic chuckle escaped. "It was great, until it wasn't."

Jonah put the snacks down. "Wanna talk about it?"

He sighed and sat in a recliner across from his best friend. "I don't even know what to say. I think she was really enjoying herself. Then I pulled into her driveway, walked her to the porch, and she ducked in and slammed the door."

Jonah narrowed his eyes and sat back. "Dude, what did you do? Scare her?"

Kevin shrugged and reached for the chips. "I don't know how. I didn't even try to kiss her. The thought crossed my mind, but she seemed nervous."

His friend slowly nodded. "Did you say anything?"

He threw another chip in his mouth as he thought. "Oh, right. I asked her to go to church with me tomorrow." Once the words tumbled out, the impact hit him as hard like one of his tackles from high school football. "Do you think I scared her off with church?"

"It's possible. Sounds like she's kind of fragile. Maybe she's mad at God."

Kevin considered Holly's past, what he knew of it. Loss of parents. Didn't reconcile with her dad before he passed away. Hadn't been thrilled to return to the mansion. He smacked his palm against his forehead. "I blew it."

"No, you're fine. Kev, you know what to do. Pray. She needs prayer. You're in her life for a reason, just like you showed up here when Lily died. You saved Nathan and me. I don't know what we would've done without you moving in."

Kevin glanced at Jonah. His friend's grief was visible, but nowhere near the bottom-of-the-canyon depth of loss Kevin found that day he knocked on their door. Similar helplessness rose like bile. He didn't feel equipped to help his friend, and he wasn't sure he could fix the mess he created with Holly. "You're right. Prayer. Trust me, moving in was a mutual rescue. I was reeling from Mallory. We all needed each other."

Jonah looked to the floor and released a deep sigh. "Sure did." He raised his head and reached for more potato chips. "We still do. I've got your back in prayer. Holly's a great girl, and I'm sure you still have a chance of building something special with her."

Kevin stood and wiped his greasy palms on his khakis. "Thanks, Jonah. I'm going to head upstairs and do some praying of my own." *For Holly. For us.*

Holly switched on the visiting room light in the mansion and sighed. The good news about her father hoarding everything was she had over a thousand ornament balls to hang from above the ceiling. She wanted to use her Sunday morning to assemble some of them in the foam-like suspended ceiling so Nathan would see, and know how to help. *It's also a good way to push away thoughts about the way my date ended. And the fact Kevin's at church and I'm not.*

She opened a few boxes and reached for her feather duster. Memories swirled with the moving dust. Metallic reds and greens her mom bought at a department store when Holly was five. Another memory surfaced. Holly, new decorations in hand, begging to help place the balls on the mansion's main tree. Her parents, arms around each other, laughing and warning her to go slow and not crowd them in the same location. *We were all happy. In the mansion. At Christmastime.*

Two hours passed. Each box reminded her of a happier time. Her parents were together and she loved being with them at the mansion. She even knew the timeframe they acquired the ornaments thanks to the style. The neon pinks and the pastels were so eighties, before she started school. The Precious Moments collection from the nineties. The whites and grays from the early aughts. Every single decoration accomplished one goal. Holly slid back into the past and totally forgot about Kevin and church.

Next, she set up the ladder and placed push pins and a box of balls on the landing. Once Holly had her supplies ready, she slowly made her way up the steps. It took over a hundred decorations before she realized Nathan's idea was coming to vision. The mix of metallics, pastels, and character balls from her view looked like a chaotic mess. From the floor, where customers would see, was a beautiful array of joy. *Just like Nathan.* She climbed the following rung so she could place a shiny silver one near a nativity-themed ornament. Images of Nathan crying punctured her tender heart as she wedged the push pin into the soft ceiling panel.

Holly's phone vibrated in her jeans, sending her into a quake that moved the box off the landing and crashing to the floor. She reached for the ladder's side and held tight with her left hand while she fished for her phone with her free hand. *Kevin.*

"Hey, Holly. Did I catch you at a bad time?"

His warm, soft voice was as comforting as a plate of chocolate chip cookies. She gripped the ladder tighter. "Um, I'm on a ladder. I wanted to get a head start on Nathan's idea."

"Are you there alone?"

"Yes, Uncle Nick's probably still at church. Why?" Her heartbeat was still way off pace.

"For one, I don't think it's a good idea to be on a ladder without someone spotting you. I'd be happy to join you and help. I could even bring lunch."

Holly raised her brows. "Why do I feel like you have more to say?"

There was a slight pause before he replied. "You're pretty perceptive, Holly Christmas."

"So? What else do you have to say?"

"If it's okay, I'd like to come over with lunch, and work with you."

Holly stared at the mirror disco ball ornament above her. *Sounds innocent enough.*

"I also want to talk about last night."

Chapter Twelve

Kevin shifted his weight as he held the hot pizza box with one hand and rang the service bell with the other. He drummed his fingers against the top of the cardboard, hoping she was on the first floor so he wouldn't have to hold their lunch much longer.

Within a minute, Holly rushed through the gift shop toward him. She wasn't smiling, but she wasn't grimacing, either. *Okay, Lord. Help me know what to do and say.* With a click of the lock, the door swung open, and he stepped inside and placed the pizza on an empty table. "Thanks for agreeing to have lunch with me."

Holly crossed her arms and turned on her heel. "I admit, it probably wasn't wise for me to put the ornaments up alone, but I don't want Uncle Nick doing it."

Okay, so she's acting cool, but not icy. "You're right. I'm happy to help." He grabbed the pizza box and jogged to catch up to her. "I do want to talk, though."

She sighed and slowed down. "Can we eat first?"

Kevin gazed at her, her eyes pleading for a reprieve. He gave a slight nod and let her lead the way.

Holly navigated through the office area and stopped next to a desk that displayed the vase of flowers he'd given her. "Is this a good place to sit?" She pointed to her desk and the one nearby he assumed was Nick's.

"Absolutely. Give me a minute to set up." He opened the box and a cheesy waft danced past his nostrils. Holly set some paper plates out and he reached for napkins he'd stashed in his back pocket. "Nothing fancy, but it smells good."

Holly's smile almost made Kevin's knees buckle. "You can't beat Mama Mia's. Best pizza around." She reached for a slice and dropped it on a plate, then repeated the process.

Kevin looked down at the food closest to him, and then pressed his lips together as he tapped his foot on the floor. He cleared his throat and glanced at Holly. "Do you mind if I say grace?"

Although the slice was in her hand, she snapped her mouth shut and closed her eyes, giving him the courage to continue with a simple table prayer.

When he finished, Holly looked up, expressionless. "Amen."

Kevin reached for his third piece of pizza before he gathered the courage to bring up their date. "I don't want you to think I'm pressuring you in any way. Did I scare you last night?"

Holly dabbed her mouth with her napkin and shook her head. "You were a perfect gentleman. Is that what you mean?"

He shrugged. "Honestly, I'm not sure. One minute we're walking to your door, and the next, you slam it and I'm by myself on the porch. Did I say something to offend you?"

She dipped a breadstick in sauce. "Not really."

Kevin arched his eyebrows. "I'm confused."

"I reacted. Overreacted. It was the invite to church. It really threw me off."

So Jonah had been right. "May I ask why it upset you?"

"This isn't easy to confess, but I haven't been to church in a very long time. Faith isn't important only to Uncle Nick, I grew up in the church, too. Our faith was very strong, or so I thought. When my mom got sick and passed away, I struggled with a lot of questions."

Kevin wiped the grease off his hands, pushed his plate back, and leaned closer to Holly. "I can imagine. Jonah went through the same thing when his wife died. Did you talk to anyone about your feelings?"

She held her breath for a moment before letting a burst of air expel. "The women weren't very nice. The last time I went was when I tried to sign up for an event and was told it was for mothers and daughters." She blinked a few times before continuing. "The pain of that moment was right up there with the news my mom was gone."

"Oh, Holly. That's terrible. No wonder you had strong emotions at the mention of church. I can't promise the people where I attend are perfect, but they are kind and welcoming. I asked too soon. I'm sorry."

She smiled, and a layer of freckles shone against her cheeks. She moved her plate away and stood. "I'm sorry, too. I should have talked about it last night."

Kevin rose and straightened as he closed the gap between them. He leaned in, eyes closed, and felt her silky hair as he put his arms around her waist. She wasted no time resting her hands on his shoulders. The kiss started tentative, but Holly slid her arms around his neck and the kiss deepened before Kevin stepped back. "I think I not only saw fireworks, but Santa flying in his sleigh."

Holly rolled her eyes and playfully hit his arm as she strolled over to the corner of Nick's desk. "Thank you for not judging me about church. It means a lot how easy it is to talk to you."

Kevin focused on getting his heartrate back to normal before stealing a glance into those knockout eyes. "Maybe those devastating times in our past has helped prepare us. I didn't think I'd ever want to date after that. Now, I'm wondering how soon can I ask you out again?"

Holly giggled. "I should be hungry again in a few hours."

Holly looked at her reflection in her bathroom mirror and smiled. She couldn't stop grinning, even when brushing her teeth for bed. The lunch with Kevin had turned into dinner. Then a movie. And a memorable kiss good night. For the first time in years, she associated the mansion with something wonderful.

She'd left the kitchen light on. As she reached for the switch, an unopened stack of business mail caught her attention. Flipping past a realtor postcard and the electric bill, she found an envelope from her parents' bank, addressed to The Christmas Mansion, forwarded to her. Holly furrowed her eyebrows and ripped the outer paper to reveal a loan coupon with a red stamp across the front.

Loan Overdue.

Chapter Thirteen

Kevin locked the school van as the students scrambled toward the mansion. Red and orange leaves covered the path to the entrance, and a brisk October breeze lifted the foliage into a quick dance before they fell to the pavement. He walked through the door, immediately scanning the room for Holly.

Nathan held a box of decorations they'd bought at the dollar store. "Miss Holly said I can help her with the ornaments today."

Kevin raised his eyebrows. "You talked to her already?"

Nathan's face puckered. "Not in person. I texted her when I woke up at five."

Kevin sighed and side-stepped the tween. "Let's see if she's in the guest room preparing it for you."

Once upstairs, they discovered boxes of decorations littering the floor and Holly in the middle, attaching hooks to glittery decorations. Her cheeks were flushed. Kevin cleared his throat to get her attention. "Is this a bad time?"

Holly looked up and held her hand to her heart. "Kevin! You guys startled me. I'm ready for help. Nathan, you still game?"

Kevin narrowed his gaze, trying to read her. Dark circles covered the freckles under her eyes.

Nathan jogged over with his box. "This looks amazing. How many bulbs are already hung?"

Holly tapped her cheek for a moment. "Take a guess."

"Two hundred?"

She smiled. "I think it's more like four hundred. I need help putting hooks on the ones that don't have them. I can use as much help as possible. There's a lot of them."

Nathan nodded. "I'll go get the others." And he was off.

Kevin moved closer to Holly, but still kept a professional distance. Her flowery perfume wafted close enough to remind him of their goodnight kiss. "Everything okay?"

Holly shrugged. "Tired. A little stressed."

"Anything you want to talk about?"

She picked up a hook but kept her focus on him. "Not yet. I need to process it first." She moved the hook and pricked her palm, shaking her hand as she dropped the sharp metal.

"Okay. How can I help?"

"The college group is on their way to work on tech stuff. Do you mind supervising them?"

Kevin backed up, but her intoxicating scent remained. "I'm on it." He started to leave, but stopped and faced her. "You can come to me about anything, Holly."

She looked down for a moment, then raised her chin in acknowledgement. "That means a lot."

Ten minutes later, Kevin sat in a control room that housed the brains to some of the old animatronic exhibits. Jessica, Ian, Adam, and Rachel were on their laptops ready to show him their progress.

Jessica pushed up her glasses. "I've been busy because the need here is so great."

Adam coughed. "Remember what Kevin and Holly keep saying. Presentation is as important as the details. A positive attitude makes all the difference when hiring."

Jessica scowled and looked at her screen. "I'm most excited about fundraising. I created a campaign to bring in monies so we can bid on Christmas-themed movie props. The mansion can be a complete tour, year-round, bringing up nostalgia from favorite movies."

Kevin squatted to look at her work. "I'm impressed. What's your process?"

Jessica turned toward him. Her smile was like finding a rare artifact. "I created a budget from the donations that came in, and then I started searching for online auctions that featured the items. There's quite a few." She held up a file. "Here are the winning bids that are about to be delivered. A signed script. I scored an entire wardrobe from that one ten years ago with all those kids. And, last, a rooftop scene complete with the Santa costume the actor wore."

Rachel moved her chair closer to Jessica. "I collected the guest books from the current one to five years ago. I put all the names and addresses in a database and sent out a postcard, letting them know we have a new website."

Kevin folded his arms against his chest. "There's a new website?"

Ian pointed toward his monitor. "We do now. I included a page for donations. Some have come in already."

Jessica picked up her phone, swiped a few screens, and looked at Kevin. "I sent a press release to the media in a one hundred-mile radius letting them know the Christmas Mansion is updating its look and is growing with the families who make this their tradition. I already have Holly scheduled for an interview tomorrow. One station even asked if Nick can be a guest on their weekly senior citizen program."

Kevin shook his head. "You guys have hit the ground running. This is amazing. Holly will be thrilled. Adam, you've been quiet. What have you been doing?"

He chuckled. "Supplied everyone with energy drinks."

Ian rolled his eyes. "You also went to every business in town asking for donations and manpower to assemble the rooms when everything is ready."

Adam slowly nodded and sat back in his chair. He squinted, straightened, and leaned over to an old sound board that had something on it. "What's this?" Adam retrieved a piece of paper.

Rachel's eyes widened. "That isn't your business."

Adam looked down at the paper and paled. "Um, Kevin, you take this. It looks important."

Bold red letters appeared in front of him with the words 'Loan Overdue.' A lead weight dropped to the bottom of Kevin's stomach. Before he could form any thoughts, a gasp came from the doorway.

Holly's lip curled to the point it resembled a snarl. "What are you doing reading my mail?"

Holly tapped her foot while she waited for Kevin to speak. He dropped the bank note as if it were on fire, and the students volleyed their stares between her and Kevin.

His words were more like a stammer. "I, wasn't. Adam found—and then—Holly. I would never betray your trust that way."

Rachel raised her hand. "It's true. Adam held it, and passed it to Kevin as you walked in."

Holly swallowed hard. "Please give it to me. I left it by mistake when I was doing some research." Her eyes searched Kevin's. A flood of warmth emanated from his gaze, which in turn softened her rigid stance.

Kevin stood and walked over, keeping his focus on her. The intensity nearly made her knees buckle. Once he handed the paper to her, their fingers grazed, igniting a spark of chemistry so strong she stepped back. "Holly, if you want to—"

Holly cut him off as fear and electricity battled for control within her. "I need to check on the others. I'll be back." She turned toward the hall, grasping the note like a lifeline. It was Adam's voice she heard as she trekked away.

"Hey, Kevin, do you and Holly have something going on? If she had stayed another minute I think we would've needed to call the fire department."

After the student groups left, Holly sat at her desk to review the paperwork Rachel had left behind. She read the same sentence about movie props three times before placing the folder back down. Although Holly was completely out of practice, she was desperate enough to close her eyes and fold her hands. *God, help me. I feel so overwhelmed. Is the mansion in trouble? What do I do?* She sank her head down and rested until the folder stuck to her forehead.

Holly sighed and started pacing. She heard footsteps heading toward her and peeked down the hall. Uncle Nick. He ambled with slumped shoulders, his appearance so unlike him that Holly trekked to him. "Are you okay? You're pale."

He stopped, shook his head, and pulled out a paper from his back pocket. "I should have said something sooner."

Chapter Fourteen

Kevin, in the Welling kitchen, cut up a hot dog and tossed the pieces in the macaroni and cheese.

Jonah set the table and tried to process what happened between Kevin and Holly. "Do you think she's mad? That she feels you betrayed her trust?"

Kevin shrugged as he mixed the cheesy hot dog combination together. "I can't stop thinking about her. The look on her face when she came in the room. She looked devastated."

Jonah sighed as he grabbed the bowl from his friend and placed it on the table. "Go to her. You hate this meal anyway. Let's be honest, only Nathan likes it."

"You're right. I want to make sure she understands I didn't pick the letter up in the first place, Adam did. I want to help if she'll let me." Kevin reached for his car keys.

Jonah peeked into the living room to call Nathan for dinner and returned to the kitchen. "I'll be praying for you. For Holly, too."

Kevin glanced at the widower. "Appreciate it. I know you don't talk a lot about missing Lily, but I still pray for you and Nathan."

Jonah offered a small smile as Nathan entered the kitchen to wash his hands. "If you happen to stop at a store on the way home, pick me up anything." Jonah pointed at the dinner. "But this."

Twenty minutes later, Kevin peeked through the mansion's front window. The tourist attraction was still open but he didn't notice any customers milling around. *Everything looks so much better since my first visit. Holly's worked so hard.* He stepped over to the front doors and pushed them open, the bell above tinkled. "Holly? It's Kevin."

"I'm in the office." Her voice sounded strangled.

He jogged down the hall to find Nick hunched over her, the two hugging. Holly grasped a tissue in her hand. “Is everything okay?”

Nick stepped back. “I’m fine explaining it all, Holly. Kevin should know.”

Holly slowly nodded and pulled out a chair. “It seems that the mansion is in a bit of a financial challenge.”

Kevin felt an ache in his chest as he took a seat. “Okay. What’s going on?”

Nick cleared his throat and looked at the floor. “Holly’s dad had so many plans for this place. More ideas than room. All the figurines and decorations the kids sorted upstairs, Chris had a vision for each piece. He wanted to renovate. Take out some walls. Update rooms. Widen a hallway. Before he approached the bank, he got sick.”

Holly dabbed her cheek with the tissue.

Nick raised his head and a couple of tears fell. “I knew it was worse than he was letting on, so I went to the bank and asked for funds. Chris signed off on it as the owner, and they let me co-sign. Thing is, when he passed away, I was stuck. I didn’t know his vision. I saw way more work than my hands could provide. The payments were due and I avoided them. It was wrong.” His voice caught and he started to sob.

Holly jumped up and wrapped her arms around him. “It’s okay, Uncle Nick. We’ll figure something out. I promise.”

Kevin shifted in the metal chair. “The bank’s looking for payment?”

Holly straightened. “I’m going there first thing in the morning. My parents were customers for decades.”

Kevin stood and moved closer to them. “I’d like to go with you.” He wasn’t sure what to expect, but her shoulders lowered and she leaned in to give him a peck on the cheek.

Nick faced him and offered a shaky hand. "You're a fine young man, Kevin Holt. Thank you for everything you've done."

"My pleasure, sir. Did you two have dinner? I'm hungry and would love to treat you both."

Holly looked to Nick, who waved her off. "You two young'uns go on. I have leftovers at home."

Kevin's heartbeat surged when he caught her gaze. "Are you sure?"

Nick chuckled. "Positive. You'll have more fun without me."

Holly wrapped a gooey strand of cheddar from her grilled cheese sandwich around her finger. The Valley Diner was close to her house and satisfied her hunger every time she visited. She giggled as she watched Kevin wipe a stain off the fading menu.

"You could've picked anywhere to eat. Are you worried about money? Sweetheart, I said I'd pay."

Holly nearly melted at the sound of him calling her that. "I love the food here. Sure, the décor is a bit outdated, but that's not what I'm paying attention to." She winked. "My focus is on you."

He swallowed and leaned in. "You're flirting with me, Holly Christmas."

Her mouth quirked upward and she reached for his hand. "I don't have words to convey how much I appreciate all you've done. Between the work the students have finished and your offer to go to the bank with me, you're not like anyone else I've met."

His thumb traced her palm. "I believe in you, and the mansion. Rachel even said she thinks we can get enough movie props in to have a grand re-opening in early December."

"This morning I woke with a thick sense of dread. There's hope now. Thank God." Her voice choked with emotion.

Kevin raised his eyebrows. "Say that again?"

Holly tilted her head to the side. "There's hope?"

He shook his head. "The thanking God part."

Holly gasped. "I wasn't even aware I said it. I never confessed atheism, I walked away from my faith is all. I still believe God is real and does good things."

"Okay. Are you ready to experience more of Him? Maybe through church?"

Her eyes widened and she held up her hand. "Whoa there, Kevin. I'm happy to end the day with some confidence about finances. I'm thrilled to be here with you. I admit God's good. I'm not at a place emotionally to proclaim God's good to *me*."

Kevin tied his black dress shoes and checked his phone. One email was from his classroom aide confirming lesson plans with the sub. The other notification was an alert. Time to pick up Holly and meet with the bank representative.

He pulled in her driveway, shaking off the tension from last night's goodbye. His heart ached knowing Holly's grief created a wall that not only protected her from hurt, but prevented her from a full relationship with her Heavenly Father. *Don't pressure her. Be supportive. She needs you.*

Holly shut the mansion door behind her and showed no emotion as she hurried down the steps toward his car. Even as Kevin greeted her and opened the door for her, she mumbled thanks and climbed in without another word.

Kevin waited until they were on the two-lane highway before speaking. "You okay?"

She offered a small smile. "A little nervous. Uncle Nick wanted to join us but I wanted to gauge the situation. He feels bad enough as it is."

"You want to return with good news."

Holly nodded.

Ten minutes later, he pulled into the parking lot and focused on those wide, green eyes. "Would it be okay if I prayed?"

She closed her eyes and folded her hands.

"Father, we thank You that You care deeply about what matters to us. The Christmas Mansion is a staple in this community and the family has worked hard to make it a wonderful attraction. Please give Holly direction with the bank today, and provision. Whatever they owe, may the bank give them favor. Fill her with peace that passes all understanding. In the name of Jesus, Amen." He glanced over. Holly swiped at her cheek as she whispered an "Amen."

"Okay. Let's go." She opened her door before he could reach her. Her pace was quick and sure as she marched through the blacktop lot and pushed on the glass doors.

A young woman in a bright red sweater who didn't look much older than Holly's college interns greeted them from behind the counter. "Good morning. How can I help you today?" She closed the heavy ledger she had been looking at and let it thump against the desk.

Holly approached her. "Hello, I have an existing loan that I need to discuss with a representative."

The associate's smile remained. "Of course. Let me call her extension." She pushed a couple buttons and held the receiver to her ear, her focus still on Holly. "Hello, I have a couple here that need to speak to you."

Kevin looked to the side where clear cubicles stood. A woman with auburn hair in some kind of bun walked toward them. With each step, layers of dread lined his stomach. Her attention was on Holly as she extended her hand, but one glance toward Kevin and she froze. Her hand dropped. She paled.

He could barely speak. "Mallory?"

Chapter Fifteen

Holly felt as if all the blood drained from her and she was a bag of bones ready to drop. The handshake she shared with the loan representative fell limp as soon as Kevin spoke the woman's name. Mallory. How many could there be?

The redhead stepped back, her focus on Kevin. "Kevin. What a surprise."

His steely gaze could have cracked cement. "I've had bigger shockers that involved you."

Yep, this is the Mallory that bailed on their wedding. Holly placed herself between them. "Is there someone else that could help?"

Mallory blinked a few times and wiped her palms against her form-fitting skirt. "I apologize. This is a small branch, and I'm the only associate working the loan department today." She attempted the handshake once more.

Holly forced a smile and a grip that would hopefully show she wasn't scared. "I'm Holly Christmas. I'm co-owner of The Christmas Mansion since my father passed away. I'd like to talk about a letter I received." She turned to Kevin. "It's okay. You can stay in the lobby."

Kevin still looked like he could transform into the Hulk at any given moment, but he nodded and strode toward the lobby, a small corner of furniture in a semi-circle.

Mallory's smile was tight-lipped, but at least she had one. She gestured for Holly to follow her to her cubicle. "Let's start over. I'm Mallory Banks. I'm sorry for your loss."

Holly studied Kevin's ex fiancée. She was every bit the business professional with her silk blouse and skirt, her tresses in a bun. If Holly had the time each morning, she could try to apply makeup as skilled as Mallory's looked, but it would be a dismal failure. At first glance the two women didn't seem to have anything in common, except Kevin. "Thank you. The mansion was everything to my father, and I'm playing catch-up as I only recently returned to Geneseo Valley." Holly opened her purse and retrieved the bank's letter, handing it over to Mallory.

Mallory picked up a pair of tortoise-shell frames and put them on before reading. She nodded and placed the paper in front of her. "This comes from corporate. It's standard after missing three payments when calls haven't worked. Let me pull the account up." She swung over to her laptop and started typing.

Holly fidgeted with her hands as she looked out the see-through walls. Kevin was flipping through a magazine with enough speed that his hair was moving. *This is a disaster*. "I didn't even know about the loan or the late payments until I received the letter."

Mallory scanned the monitor. "It looks like corporate left voicemails on Nicholas Christmas' phone?"

Holly closed her eyes and sucked in a breath before opening them. "I know this is an excuse, but I want you to understand the complete situation. My uncle's a senior citizen, and until I returned, he was trying to keep the mansion open and renovate it. Uncle Nick was grieving his brother's death. It isn't right, I understand, but he put this on the back burner."

Mallory pushed her chair away from the computer and took her glasses off, facing Holly. "With interest, the loan amount now due is eight thousand dollars, plus the monthly payments already arranged."

Holly gasped and rubbed her temples. "I don't have that."

"There are many options before worst case scenarios. My job is to explore them with you."

Nausea rolled through Holly like a tsunami. "What's the worst case?"

Mallory's voice was gentle, but her gaze was all business. "The bank would take possession." She cleared her throat. "Miss

Christmas. Holly. We aren't even close to that decision. I've encountered much worse situations than this one that have found a resolution that pleased everyone. Let me take some time to create options and we'll meet again in a few days. Does that sound good?"

Holly felt like a child being consoled over a deflated balloon. "Thank you."

Mallory stood and walked to the archway leading back to the teller and lounge areas. Holly jumped up and followed, her heart still racing. Mallory turned to shake hands one last time, her hands moist. "By any chance, will Kevin be joining you for the next appointment?"

Kevin didn't dare speak first as he opened both the bank doors, and then his car, for Holly. He put the key in the ignition and snuck a peek at her olive skin. Her grip on the bank folder was strong enough the papers on top creased.

"I was right. I knew it." Her words flew out like a nail gun.

He turned toward her. "What? I apologize for my behavior. I was completely caught off—"

Her green eyes blazed. "I prayed, Kevin. I did. What happened? I meet your ex fiancée, who is in charge of my future, and I owe over eight thousand dollars."

A sledgehammer of pain hit his heart. *She blames God.* "Honey, this looks bad, but all things are possible. I can stay away from here if you want, or, I can even face my feelings and deal with Mallory. Whatever helps you. Honest."

Holly hit the dashboard. "She was fine. It's the money. Where am I going to come up with that kind of cash?" She rubbed her temples. "I have a terrible headache. I need to go home and think in complete darkness."

Kevin nodded and started the engine. Silence enveloped them for three miles. He glanced over and saw her wipe the side of her cheek. "What can I do?"

Holly shook her head. "God is not good. He can't be. My parents are gone. They died thinking I hated the mansion and Christmas. You and I seem to have something great starting and then we run into Mallory. Then the debt. I'm a cosmic joke."

Lord, help me here. "I don't have the answers, but I know truth. God doesn't lie. You are not a punch line. God does take all things and turn them to good. I believe that. I believe in you. I believe Him."

He pulled into her driveway and with her earlier speed, she jumped out before he could race to her and open her door. "Holly. Please don't shut me out."

She stalked up the steps and jammed her key in the hole.

Kevin jogged to catch up to her. Before she unlocked the door, he reached out and turned her toward him. "We have something great here, and I want to be a part of your life. Please let me help you."

She felt limp in his grip. "I don't even know where to start."

"Let's take this one step at a time so it isn't as overwhelming."

Holly nodded. "She's going to call with a few options for payment."

Kevin smiled and squeezed her arm. "See? That's positive news."

Her mouth turned up, if only for a moment as she fell into his chest and grabbed onto his shirt like a lifeline. "You're right. I'm sorry I was so negative. It's hard to say. I'm scared."

Chapter Sixteen

A week later, Holly's heels echoed off the wooden flooring throughout the hallway as she trekked to the guest room on the second floor. Kevin's students spent two days hanging the last of the suspended ornaments from the guest room ceiling.

Nathan sprung from behind a partition before she reached the entry. "Close your eyes. I'm going to walk you inside."

Holly obeyed, partly to focus on getting her heartrate under control after it jumped twenty points after his scare. "I don't have a lot of time. Kevin and I are going to the bank once your substitute brings the van around."

A sticky hand encircled hers. "This won't take long. Get ready to be amazed."

She chuckled as he led her into the room. After a few more steps, Nathan let go.

"Okay. Open your eyes. You might even need sunglasses." Nathan's friends snickered.

Holly took a deep breath and opened her eyes. The entire ceiling was full of ornaments. Golds, silvers, pastels, clear, gaudy, circles, squares, spirals, hundreds, if not a thousand bulbs glittered while the kids beamed with pride. "This is the most beautiful thing I've ever seen."

Kevin stepped forward so he was next to her, his intoxicating cologne swirled around her nostrils. He touched her shoulders and shifted her to the opposite side of the room. "Look over here."

An archway, all adorned with ornaments. Holly walked through and came across two narrow, side-by-side red, vinyl cushions. They reminded her of punching bags, but square and wider. She raised her eyebrows. "What's this?"

Kevin's smile was as bright as the decorations. "Walk through it. It won't be easy."

Holly tried to march straight through, but got caught. More laughter. “Alright. I’ll try sliding through this way.” She moved to her side and inched through.

Nathan raced past the archway to the cushions. “It’s Santa’s chimney!”

Holly squeezed out and walked around it. She lifted her hand and Nathan mimicked her, the two enjoying a high-five. “You’ve all done an outstanding job. More than I could ever have dreamed.”

Kensi peeked from behind Kevin’s shadow. “You like it?”

Holly strolled over to the tween with long blonde locks. “I love it.”

Uncle Nick entered the room and whistled. “This is a show-stopper. You guys created a masterpiece.”

Nathan jiggled with excitement. “When can other kids try it?”

Kevin cleared his throat. “Miss Jessica from the college is working on more Christmas movie items. Another student has a construction team donating their time once everything is delivered to set it all up.”

Holly released a shaky breath. “My hope is to have a huge celebration so families can see everything and enjoy it to kick off their Christmas season.”

Nick pushed his hand into the pretend chimney. “Are you still shooting for early December?”

She nodded and focused on Kevin. “If the bank lets me.”

An hour later, Holly’s stomach growled as she waited in the bank lounge for Mallory to call her in. Kevin tapped his foot as he leafed through a magazine. She thought about the guest room and all the students and their smiles. Still, her hands shook.

Kevin returned the periodical and leaned in. “You okay?”

She swallowed hard. “Nervous. Hungry.”

He placed his hand on top of hers. “We’ll grab something when we’re done here if you want.”

"Let's see how this goes. I might not want to eat at all."

Kevin stood as soon as Mallory came into view. He gripped his hand into a ball and released it as she strode closer. Her ginger tresses were in a high ponytail and her jade-colored suit brought out the green in her eyes. Her attention was on Holly, but he caught Mallory's eyes darting toward him.

Holly rose and whispered, "Here we go."

Mallory gestured for the two to take a seat opposite her cluttered desk. Kevin shook off the wedding day memories as he waited for both women to sit. Shame and anger crept through him like an invisible fog. *Help me, Father. I don't want to be bitter any longer. I want to be supportive for Holly.*

Holly spoke first. "Is there any positive news you can give me?"

Mallory opened her folder and rested her hands on the desk. "I believe so. I had a couple meetings with my bosses out of the regional offices and like me, they want to make this work. Your recent move and attempt to reach me helped. I have a copy of the options for you." She reached into the green file and handed Holly a stack of papers clipped together.

Mallory's eyes locked with his as Holly perused the first page. "Sorry, I only made one copy."

He raised his hands. "That's fine. She's the co-owner." *Thank you, Lord. I was civil. Keep giving me strength.*

Holly flipped the paper while Mallory turned to her computer and typed.

Kevin started to strum his fingers on the armrest, but both shot him a narrow gaze. He cleared his throat and moved toward Holly. "So?"

Holly held up her index finger as she read the last page. After thirty seconds, she placed everything on the desk and faced him. "If I understand correctly, there are three payment plans to choose from. A monthly bill that factors in both the loan and the overdue amount. A quarterly option that does the same, but the money due would be more. Finally, a one-time payment that would take care of the late payments and keep the loan current." She glanced at Mallory. "Is that correct?"

Mallory stopped typing and nodded. "Do you have any questions?"

Holly shifted in her chair. "Could I go somewhere private and call my uncle? I'd like to discuss it with him."

"Of course. I'll take you to the conference room. Kevin, you can stay here if you want."

Holly left with her gaze straight ahead as she followed Mallory, leaving Kevin alone. He lowered his head. "Okay God, You've brought Holly and me through this much, please help us as we finish up here. Give Holly and Nick wisdom as they seek the right plan for the mansion. Fill me with peace and forgiveness as I fight memories. You're the Way Maker, and I give You all the glory. Amen."

"Kevin? Were you just praying?"

He turned to find Mallory standing behind him. He jumped from his seat and raked his hand through his hair. "Sorry, I didn't know you were there. I can go in the waiting area."

She held up her hand, revealing manicured nails with a green polish. "Actually, I was hoping you would be in here when I returned. We need to talk."

Chapter Seventeen

Every muscle in Kevin's body tensed as Mallory sat in the chair Holly had vacated, pulling it closer. He was certain his heartbeat was louder than the oldies station they were playing in the lobby. "Mallory, we don't need to talk. I don't have anything to say, and you summed things up with your letter I received on our wedding day."

Mallory shook her head with enough force to make her ponytail dance. "That's just it. You deserve so much more than I was able to give. In that letter. On that day. Now." She choked up, paused, and smoothed her hands against her skirt before continuing. "I am so sorry for abandoning you. I should have said something long before then. I humiliated you, caused you a lot of debt, and hurt you deeply. Please forgive me."

Kevin searched her eyes for any hint of deception, but all he noticed were the flecks of gold that attracted him to her years ago. He deeply inhaled and held the breath for a moment. *I think I've asked for more help from You today than I have since I realized how much I needed you in my life.* He expelled the air and fidgeted. "I didn't expect this. Was it true, what you wrote? That there was someone else?"

She pursed her lips together and shook her head. "Kevin, I was terrified. I wasn't ready to be a wife. I was so immature and selfish. I panicked. My thinking was if you thought I was with someone else, you wouldn't try to find me and change my mind."

He nodded slowly. "You were right. I hated you. It took me a long time not to picture you laughing at me, while with someone else."

"That never happened. I didn't find anything humorous about what I did. I still don't. When you came in here last week, I thought I'd crawl under my desk. Any confidence I have in my job doesn't mean anything when I have to face my past."

Kevin looked out the glass partition but didn't see Holly. He glanced at Mallory. "What changed?"

She leaned back. "Faith. One of my classmates from college noticed how emotionally unstable I was my last semester. She invited me to her church, and I went. Believed God loved me enough, even after all I'd done, to give His Son as my Savior. After graduation, I moved back to town and found a church in Mount Morris. My relationship with Christ gave me the grace to forgive myself. Now, it would mean a lot if you could do the same."

Holly sat in one of the plush chairs with wheels as she waited for Uncle Nick to answer the phone. The third ring switched over to voicemail, so she hung up. *Maybe he's working on an exhibit and doesn't hear it. A second call might work.* She pressed re-dial and sighed. Voicemail again. She groaned. "C'mon, Uncle Nick. I need you."

After Holly returned the phone to the cradle, she reflected in the quiet atmosphere. The options were fair, but only the first one seemed doable. Even that would make things quite tight financially. At a time when the mansion could use an increase in funds. *Perhaps Mallory will let me think about it so I can talk with Uncle Nick and Kevin.* Holly spun in the chair before standing and navigating her way back to Mallory's office.

She peeked at the lobby clock and realized Kevin had been stranded with Mallory for a few minutes. Her pace increased as she entered the lobby and turned toward the clear cubicles. Kevin was still in his chair, but Mallory was across from him. *That can't be good.* Holly's pace was at a power-walk level when she burst through the entry.

Kevin's gentle tone seemed to float through the office space. "Mallory, of course I forgive you. I'll also definitely take you up on that offer. I'd love to check out your church."

Chapter Eighteen

Holly's knees nearly buckled as she watched the two former lovebirds stand and hug without seeing her. She coughed and Kevin dropped his arms and backed up as if Mallory were on fire. *If she isn't, I am.*

Mallory turned around, smiled, and sauntered to her own chair. "Were you able to reach your uncle?"

Holly's throat felt like sandpaper. "No, it went to voicemail. Do you need a decision today? I'd really like to discuss it with him." She glanced at Kevin, who showed no expression at all.

There wasn't any hesitation, nothing that suggested Holly walked in on something, when Mallory replied. "If you could get back to me by Friday, that would be perfect. You have my card, that has my number and email, if that's more convenient."

Holly nodded and reached for her purse, gripping the handles until her knuckles turned ghost-white. "Thank you for your help. I definitely will be in touch." She stepped into the hall, fixated on seeing how Kevin would exit Mallory's domain.

He ambled toward Holly, but stopped and turned toward Mallory. "Take care. I appreciate everything you said."

"Talk to you soon, Kevin. Goodbye, Holly."

Holly was at a near jog as she exited the bank and rushed to the car.

Kevin sounded breathless as he caught up to her and unlocked the doors. "Everything okay?"

She bit at her lip for a moment. "You tell me. Just what's going on between you and Mallory?"

Kevin furrowed his eyebrows as he searched Holly's wide, frantic eyes. "I'm confused. I joined you at this meeting to support you."

Holly shoved the bank folder into her tote and tapped her foot while Kevin opened the door for her. "Then we're both unsure. I thought you were here for me, but when I reached earshot of you two, the conversation seemed pretty intimate."

Kevin sat in the driver's seat and turned toward her. "It was friendly, and that's an answer to prayer. Sweetie, you have no idea the pain I felt when she left me at the altar. It took me three years to even look at another woman as someone I'd consider marrying. That's you, Holly."

She stared straight ahead, jaw set. "You're going to church with her."

He sighed. *So that's what this is about*. "She invited me. As a friend. That's it. Did you hear what I said before? I have feelings for you. When I think about the future, your face comes to mind."

Holly didn't budge. "I wasn't left at the altar, but I know abandonment as well. I'm scared to death of it happening again." She shifted slightly toward him, her cheeks moist.

His arm rested on her shoulder. "This is different. Today was closure for me. Mallory means nothing to me. What you experienced was grief. You lost your parents. They didn't abandon you."

Holly shook her head as a sob escaped. "You don't understand. I'm not worried about you leaving me."

He kept his arm on her, massaging the area in a small circle. "What is it then? Help me understand."

She turned with enough strength that he lost his grip on her. Her eyes lasered into his. "Kevin. I'm afraid I'll be the one to check out. I'm dealing with renovations, two groups of students, the bank, Uncle Nick, missing my dad, falling for you, and fear because of what I felt in my gut when I saw you with Mallory, smiling."

Kevin blinked and studied her. *She's serious. And I don't know what to say.*

He reached her driveway and turned off the ignition. "It's fear. You're scared to enter a relationship. It's okay. I'm afraid, too. But not enough to back away from it."

Her hand reached for the door handle and stayed there. "You and Mallory have a history, and with this forgiveness and a church invite between you, I can't compete with that." She clicked the lever and climbed out. "Honestly? I don't know if I want to. I'm sorry."

Kevin jumped out and raced after her. "Holly, let's talk. This is crazy."

Holly stopped and shot a glare that could have cracked the sidewalk. "It isn't to me. I need time to think. Please, just go home. I'll call you later."

He opened his mouth to respond, but nothing came out. He extended his hand to touch her, but she moved so fast he was swatting air. His back stiffened at the sound of a door slam, leaving him alone. Again.

Holly threw her bag on the couch and fell on the cushion next to it. *What have I done?* Lines etched on Kevin's forehead the moment she demanded he step away stayed with her as she buried her face in a pillow. *I overreacted. The loan stress got to me. That's it. Mallory's harmless. If she was evil she would demand full payment on the loan.* Holly lifted herself off the pillow and slid off the couch until she was in a standing position. "Okay, Kevin. I'm coming to apologize." Her tentative steps became a sprint as she returned to her front door, unhooked the latch, and switched the lock off. She opened her mouth as she turned the knob, ready to grovel. "Kevin, I'm so—Kevin?" Holly glanced around and stumbled to a halt. He'd left. Just like she'd demanded.

Chapter Nineteen

Jonah clicked off the television remote and threw a couch pillow at Kevin. "Dude. You've been moping around here for two weeks. it's obvious you miss her. "

Kevin pushed the soft, red square for the living room onto the floor. "You haven't seen Holly. She's serious. Her last words to me were to wait for her to call." He pulled out his phone from his pocket and held it up. "See? No call."

"Has she even spoken to you when the kids visit The Christmas Mansion?"

Kevin shook his head. "She's had Uncle Nick be her mouthpiece. It's awkward. The students know something's going on. What am I supposed to do? She's afraid either Mallory and I are meant for each other, or Holly's own brokenness will cause her to leave me at the altar. An altar that doesn't exist. She created a preemptive breakup to avoid the future abandonment."

Jonah whistled. "I'm sorry. Fear does crazy things."

"How do I bounce back from this? Everything was going great. Even Mallory asked for forgiveness. Now I feel more alone than ever."

Nathan flew into the room and dove next to Kevin. "Who are you talking about?"

Kevin moved down to give Nathan more room. "Miss Holly."

"Don't worry about her. You'll see her soon." Nathan punched him playfully on the arm.

Jonah and Kevin exchanged looks and shrugged before the tween jumped up. "Forgot my drink. Be right back."

Jonah turned the television on again. "What's he talking about?"

Kevin stood and headed for the kitchen. "I'm his teacher. You're his dad."

Holly sighed as she screwed a new bulb into a strand of white lights. Nothing.

Uncle Nick chuckled and took the strand from her and placed it in the broken pile. “At least we’re finding this out today and not on Black Friday.”

She picked up another line of lights and plugged them in. Success. “True. Do you really think the mansion will be ready? Thanksgiving’s less than a week away.”

He reached for the strand and wrapped them around one of the six artificial trees they were decorating. “The college kids have been working every spare moment on the prop exhibit. That’s your showpiece. Add the guest room’s suspended ornaments and chimney challenge, this place is going to come alive.”

Holly placed her hands on her hips and inspected their work. Their current tree with the theme of retro toys with anything dating from the 1940’s to 1990’s, had color, sound, and memories. She straightened a sock monkey decoration. “That makes me feel better. I had to raise admission to cover the new loan payments.” She looked to the floor. “It’s doable, but I feel bad. Dad always dreamed he could find a way to have the place open for free.”

Uncle Nick released a belly laugh. “Your father was a dreamer. He had a huge heart, but some of his plans didn’t quite get off the ground. You do remember cleaning the upstairs, right?”

Images of broken decorations and half-created exhibits that never saw the light of day filled her memory. So did the early fall mornings when Nathan and Kevin helped clear all her father’s projects out.

Kevin. *I miss him.*

Her uncle nudged her in the arm. “Daydreaming?”

She avoided his gaze and paid attention to the "Life" game spinner decoration resting on top of a box, ready to place on a lower branch. "Not really."

Another tap followed by a new package of lights to test from their storage basement. "Why don't you call him? Ask him to Thanksgiving? You don't want to spend your day with me."

Holly looked up as her forehead creased. "I absolutely do. I ran from my family for too long. I can't wait to make dinner for you."

The front door bell chimed as Holly plugged the last of the lights in. "I'll get it. These work, so the toy tree should be ready to place by the window. Then we can bring the box over and decorate."

She scurried down the hall and found Nathan in the gift shop. She glanced around for Kevin, her heartbeat accelerating, but he wasn't there, nor did Nathan's dad seem to be with him. "Nathan? What's going on? Are you here alone?"

He nodded and stuffed a piece of cardstock in her hand. "I made it in school."

She turned it over and saw the turkey graphics in each corner, as well as a fancy calligraphy font in bold black letters inviting her and Uncle Nick to Thanksgiving dinner. "This is a beautiful invitation. Does your dad know about it? Or Kevin?"

Nathan looked at the wall and shrugged. "Gotta go. I have to catch the bus. You'll be there, right?"

Holly scanned the card to learn the time. "Of course. Nathan?" The door chimed again, and closed with a thud, leaving her speaking to air. "Thanks."

She returned to the tree set-up and showed Uncle Nick the customized card. "I guess you're spared my cooking. I've been so busy I didn't even buy a turkey, so that's good."

The lines around his eyes tightened as he smiled. "What did I tell you? Kevin misses you. I think this will be a wonderful Thanksgiving."

Kevin opened the potholder drawer and retrieved a pair of gloves for the oven. "Jonah, the turkey's done. What's next in Lily's recipe book?" He glanced over and caught his friend holding the treasured book to his chest. "You okay over there?"

Jonah jerked to attention and nearly dropped the handwritten recipes his wife started keeping when she was a teen. "Sorry. Looking at her words, making these foods, I miss her." He returned to the turkey page and glanced to the next recipe. "Her mashed potatoes are almost done. Nathan likes to cut the celery and put cream cheese on them, that's next. I guess you can get the dinner rolls out and prep them for the oven."

Kevin's face puckered. "Cream cheese and celery? That's different."

Jonah chuckled. "I thought so too when I went to her parent's house that first Thanksgiving. But it was her family tradition." He choked on his words. "I can't imagine not following them."

Kevin's heart ached. Rejection felt like a vacuum that sucked up his energy and resolve. Grief? A constant drain on energy, hope, and emotions. "She would be proud of what a great job you're doing with this dinner. And Nathan. I'll start the rolls."

Nathan slid into the kitchen wearing a long-sleeve Bills shirt and sweats, complete with matching socks that seemed to give him extra glide on the linoleum. "Time for celery? Is it almost dinner time?"

Jonah handed him the bag of produce. "It's time for cream cheese and celery. I can't believe you're hungry. I just told you to stop eating blueberries half an hour ago."

Nathan took the green veggies and sauntered to the sink. "I'm not hungry. Well, not that hungry. I wanted to make sure I timed it right."

Kevin raised his eyebrows. “Timed what right?”

Jonah crossed his arms. “Bud, what’s going on?”

The doorbell chimed the beginning notes of *Amazing Grace*. Nathan dropped a stalk, turned off the water, and raced down the hall.

Kevin turned to Jonah. “I think I’ll see what he’s up to.”

He picked up his pace as he heard voices. When he reached the wide-open front door, there was Nathan greeting Nick Christmas, who held a pie. Before Kevin could speak, footsteps came closer from outside.

Holly stepped inside and halted next to Nick, her smile wide. “Nathan, I hope you’re ready to eat. I made two pumpkin pies.”

Chapter Twenty

Holly's smile froze as soon as she stepped inside Jonah's foyer. The temperature inside seemed to drop. She shivered. Kevin raked a hand through his hair.

Jonah cleared his throat. "Hello? Um, Nathan? Do you have something you want to say?"

The men have no idea we were invited. Oh, no. "I apologize. I asked Nathan if you two were aware of his invitation but he had to leave. I assumed, and—" She turned to Uncle Nick. "We should go."

Nathan stepped between her and Kevin. "I know you two miss each other. Dad, you told me to always look for opportunities to be kind. This is nice, right? Telling them to leave would be mean, correct?"

Holly noticed Uncle Nick bit his lip before a laugh escaped. She sighed. The tween was an absolute delight, but quite a handful. *This could not be more awkward.*

Jonah faced Kevin. "He has a great point. Inviting others to share Thanksgiving dinner is a beautiful gesture. Lily would be furious if I ever turned anyone away."

Kevin looked up, his eyes locking with hers. "You're right." He glanced at Nathan. "Even about missing Holly."

Her hands began to shake. "I should put the pie down."

Jonah extended his hands. "Come in, please. I'm sorry for the confusion. Let me take the pie. Kevin, can you take the other one? Nathan, how about you hang coats?"

"No problem. Then I'll get my place cards I made. Kevin, you get to sit next to Holly."

Holly sucked in a breath and all of her courage. *How can I keep my love for Kevin treading when I feel like they are about to consume me?*

Fifteen minutes later, all the fixings were on the table, everyone had washed their hands, and they were in their seats. Jonah opened his arms, palms out. "It wouldn't be Thanksgiving without sharing why we are thankful. Can we each go around the room, and then I'll say Grace." He initiated reaching for the hands next to him.

Holly closed her eyes as soon as Kevin's hand encircled hers with a squeeze. Her worries about their future vanished as his hold felt secure.

Nathan's voice squawked as he shared, but he didn't let the adolescent issue deter him. "I'm thankful for everything my dad does for me. I know it's hard. He makes it look easy, though."

Holly heard a sniffle before she opened her eyes and watched Jonah try to regain composure.

Uncle Nick's eyes twinkled as he looked around the table. "I'm thankful that God still answers prayer. Last year I was a lonely man wanting to see positive changes. Here we are."

Nathan wiggled in place. "I still have more to say."

"Son, let the others go and we'll come back to you."

Kevin's velvety voice gave Holly the urge to fall into his side and rest on his shoulder. "I'm thankful for God's promises and His faithfulness. For wonderful friends. And for a future I believe will be filled with His peace." He squeezed her hand again as he cocked his head to her side.

She took a slow breath in before exhaling and sharing. "I'm thankful for second chances. I'm so glad to be back in Geneseo Valley. At the mansion. With Uncle Nick." She looked up and noticed Kevin's long eyelashes. "With each of you."

Jonah's eyes were red, tears spilling down his cheeks. "This Thanksgiving is everything to me. It means so much to have a healthy son at my side. My best friend living here to help me out, and teaching Nathan at school. I appreciate the new friends I've made with both Nick and Holly. Lily loved The Christmas Mansion, so I'm really excited about all God has planned for the place." He winked. "And for each of you. Heavenly Father, we give these praises to You. You are a good Father, and You have met our needs more than we even know. Bless everyone at this table. Bless the food and the hands that prepared it. May today's conversation bring You glory. In Christ's love, Amen."

Holly felt one more squeeze as she said amen, and then her hands were at her side as Nathan was the first to reach for the food. She eyed the mashed potatoes, her weakness.

Kevin nudged her in the arm. "You look ready to drool over those potatoes."

Holly widened her eyes as the heat rushed to her forehead. "It's a favorite, I won't lie."

Nathan stacked another piece of celery with cream cheese on his plate. "This was what my mom ate every Thanksgiving. Her job as a little girl was to spread the cheese on each piece. Now it's my chore."

Uncle Nick took a piece for himself. "It looks delightful. Did you have any other jobs?"

Nathan shrugged. "To stay out of the way."

Holly wasn't sure where she put all the food but after two helpings of turkey, potatoes, stuffing, and a piece of pie, she needed to move. "I don't know a lot about sports, but I know there's football on. You all go on out, I'll take care of the dishes. It's the least I can do for surprising you today."

Everyone stood, but Kevin ambled over to the sink. "I'll help."

Uncle Nick, Jonah, and Nathan retreated to the living room without saying a word.

Holly started gathering used silverware. "You don't have to."

He replied before she finished. "I want to." He walked over to her, invading every zone that led to her personal space.

She gasped. "Kevin…"

He wrapped his arms around her waist and pulled her to his chest. He lowered his head to her, his tender kiss searching her quivering lips. Her mouth parted to speak, but only a groan escaped. She felt love burst from head to toe as she deepened the kiss.

Kevin broke off first, stepping back with a surprised grin. “Holly. You leave me speechless.”

Holly held her hands to her mouth, and then anchored her right hand against her forehead. “I can’t believe I let that happen.”

He took her hand, massaged her wrist, and walked her to the sink where he turned on the water, added the plug, and the soap. “I’m glad. Don’t fight this, Holly. The last few weeks have been miserable. Don’t deny it. We have something worth exploring.”

She nodded. “I’m afraid you’ll discover the real me isn’t that lovable and we won’t last, not even as friends.”

Kevin’s head shook hard enough his hair moved. “That’s not going to happen. God wouldn’t let it. I feel like I do know the real you. I love who I see.”

Holly’s knees nearly buckled. “I don’t want to hurt you. I wounded my parents by leaving. You’ve been heartbroken before.”

He gently pushed a stray hair away from her face. “I trust God with us.” He lifted her chin. “Do you?”

She stood on her tip-toes to deliver another kiss and share her answer when Jonah burst in. “Call 9-1-1. Nick’s slurring his words and seems confused. I think he’s having a stroke.”

Chapter Twenty-One

Kevin watched as Holly paced the ER lobby and hallway leading to the doors where Nick was receiving treatment. He stood and tried for the third time in the two hours they'd been there, to join her.

She marched from worn carpet to concrete. "Why aren't they coming out? Someone should be giving me an update by now."

"Do you want me talk to the front desk again? Get you a coffee?"

Holly shook her head. "No, it would only worsen my nerves."

He swallowed hard as they approached the sign for the chapel. "Do you want to go and pray?"

She froze and shot him a glare. "You're kidding, right?"

Kevin sighed. "I could go alone, if you want."

She crossed her arms tight against her chest, shoulders squared. "You don't understand. I was ready, back at Jonah's, to tell you I was ready to trust God. I couldn't even get the words out before this happened. God is good? What a joke. I'm done, Kevin. Done."

Each word crushed his hopes for their future together. "Oh, Holly. That's not how God works."

"I made myself clear. No faith talk. Don't push me. I'm finished." She gave an about-face and marched onto the cold floor, leaving his heart shattered.

Okay, God. Show me what to do. Kevin's heavy steps moved in the opposite direction. One move forward added to another until he stood in front of the chapel doors.

Surrender everything. Trust Me.

Kevin spread his arms on the doors before pushing on them, heaviness taking his emotions, limbs, and joints. He drifted toward the front, knees bending the closer he reached the thick wooden table with an open, oversized Bible in the center. "I don't understand, God. She was ready to believe You are good. She's so angry. Help me make sense of this. Please let Nick be okay."

Hallway footsteps were the only sound. He ran out of words and stayed in a kneeling position, head resting on the pages as he cried. "Please. Help."

Holly's stomach knotted the longer she waited for a doctor in the private lounge. Feet swollen, she sunk in the metal chair and rested her face in her hands, tears falling in between her fingers.

Footsteps came closer and the padding in the chair next to her expelled air. "Miss Christmas? I'm Doctor Newhouse."

Holly lifted her head and straightened. "How is Uncle Nick?"

His face showed no expression, just a forehead full of creased lines. "He's awake and coherent. We have reason to believe he experienced a transient ischemic attack, commonly known as a TIA."

Holly gasped. "Is that a stroke?"

He shook his head. "It's been referred to as an early stroke, but we're trying to change it to warning stroke as that's more accurate. We're waiting for an MRI to check brain tissue. He's had an ECG and we didn't find any heart blockage, which is an excellent sign."

She held her hands together to keep them from shaking. "Is he going to be okay?"

The doctor's phone beeped. He glanced at it, clicked at it, and stood. "We're going to admit him as we wait on tests. The majority of TIA patients I treat end up with medication and some lifestyle adjustments. It's important he see his primary doctor as a full-blown stroke can take place since he's had a mini-one. Of all the scenarios, your uncle experienced a positive situation."

Holly expelled a sob. "Can I see him?"

Dr. Newhouse checked his watch. "Someone will get you once he's settled in his room. I'll be in tomorrow to check on him. Good night, Miss Christmas."

She put her hand over her heart, feeling the accelerated beat. *This is good news. He's going to be okay.* Her stomach growled and she glanced at the black-rimmed clock on the wall. Nearly midnight. No wonder. Thanksgiving dinner had been early afternoon. *Maybe there's a vending machine.* She stood, ready to walk a normal pace and find sustenance.

She turned down the hall and headed toward the cafeteria. Her focus forward, a door opened to her left, someone exiting as she passed. Holly's eyes darted over to the taller figure. Kevin.

Holly's throat went dry as his eyes searched hers. Before she could share an update or take back her lashing, Kevin stepped to the side, turned, and walked away. Holly found a wall and slumped against it. The ache inside her grew in such intensity she felt hollow. She swiped at her tears with the back of her hand. *Look at your life. Uncle Nick's in the hospital. Kevin won't look at you. The mansion is in debt. Good going.* Her heart seemed to slam against her ribcage as pain swelled within her. Holly looked to her left where she'd passed Kevin.

Every life is redeemable.

Holly glanced around, eyes wide. The words dropped into her mind like a download. No one was around to speak to her, she knew she hadn't uttered it. But the sentence pushed all her grief and regret to the side. She stood and turned away from the cafeteria path and re traced her steps to where Kevin had come from. *The chapel.*

She pushed on the wooden door and stood in the back, eyeing the Bible on the front table. The open Book drew her in like a magnet. Holly moved forward, each step feeling lighter the closer she came to the heavy table. She leaned over the open pages, reaching for them. Soft. Thin. The words at the bottom small enough she bent down further to inspect them. A phrase jumped out at her.

I am dark, but lovely.

She fell to her knees as she whispered the words. "Okay, God. You have my attention. You know my fear. You know how deeply I hurt my parents, and now Kevin. I know my words wounded You. What does every life is redeemable mean? Why am I looking at these words about being lovely?"

A deep voice from the back stopped her. "It means no matter what you've done, what you've said or thought, no matter how badly you've missed the mark, you're worth saving. Jesus would go to the Cross again, just for you. You're beautiful to Him, and you can place your trust in Christ."

Holly gasped and squinted. Could she identify the speaker as they came closer? It was an older man with tan pants and a button-down shirt who could be anyone's grandfather. "I'm sorry. Who are you?"

He reached the front and extended his hand. "Phil Sawyer. I'm the chaplain for the hospital, but I also am the pastor at New Life. I didn't mean to startle you. I was in the back praying when you came in."

Holly shook his hand. "I didn't mean to intrude. It sounds weird, but I felt like I had to come in here. I had this thought come to me about all lives being redeemable. Then this open page had the verse about being dark, but lovely. I'm full of confusion and questions."

He gestured toward the front pew, and they both sat. "Curiosity brings a lot of people through these doors. So does fear. Doesn't matter, Jesus meets us right where we're at. Are you visiting family here?"

She nodded. "My uncle. He's the only family I have left. They think it was a mini stroke. I'm waiting to see him."

The older pastor sighed. "I'm sorry to hear that."

"My boyfriend came with me for support, but I pushed him aside because I was afraid. I've hurt people before. My fear was so great that I ended up doing exactly what I dreaded. He wouldn't even look at me. I rejected his faith. I've made a mess of things."

He chuckled. "We all have. You may have rejected your friend's faith, but as long as you're breathing, you can have faith of your very own. It doesn't mean you're never going to mess up, but it brings about a love that goes beyond definition. A peace I'll never be able to explain. And direction no map could ever give you."

Holly tilted her head. "You described how Kevin and Uncle Nick live."

Pastor Sawyer took out a small book from his back pocket. "Always carry a Bible with me. Would you like me to show you how to know the Savior that makes us all look lovely?"

Chapter Twenty-Two

Kevin pulled the hospital's metal-back chair closer to Nick's bed. "You look a lot better than last night. If you didn't want pie, you could have said something." Kevin winked.

Nick's hearty laugh bounced off the sterile walls. "Trust me, this seems more like a Black Friday experience than any Christmas shopping would be. Is Holly doing okay at the mansion?"

Pangs of guilt stabbed at Kevin's conscience. "I'll go there next."

Nick narrowed his gaze. "Wanna talk about it? I'm not going anywhere."

The man's humor was incredible. "I'm confused is all. Holly took your illness hard. She was ready to trust God with everything. Then, she blamed Him. I also think she thought I was at fault as well. I received a pretty final goodbye from her."

Nick sat up in the bed and cinched the sheets around him. "You let that stop you? Don't quit on Holly Christmas. She's got layers of hurt God's taking care of. I believe you're part of His plan."

Kevin looked to the floor. *God asked me to surrender to Him. I guess He didn't mean surrender Holly altogether.* He swallowed hard. "Uncle Nick, I love her."

Another warm chuckle. "Son, tell me something I don't know. Like when are they going to let me go home?"

An hour later, Kevin cruised into the last parking lot spot in the mansion lot and whistled. Light flakes started to fall as he jogged to the sidewalk and up the steps to the entrance. A line ended right inside, chatter filling the gift shop. He spotted Adam heading his way with a batch of stickers.

"Kevin. It's about time. Everyone's here but you, and Uncle Nick, of course. The tours are full. People love the new exhibits. The news team from Rochester even came and interviewed Holly."

Kevin straightened at the mention of Holly's name, looking around to see if he could locate her. Maybe steal her away for a few moments to confess his feelings. All he found was an energetic crowd full of strangers. "How can I help?"

Adam looked at the stickers and thrust them into Kevin's hand. "Make sure each person in line gets one." He started to walk away, but stopped. "If they visit Brownie's Subs today and have their sticker on, they receive 10% off."

Kevin studied the stickers with an illustration of the mansion on the front with "Admit One." Most likely a creation from the college group. He looked at the line and smiled. Time to get to work.

When he reached the last of the stickers, he trekked up front to the register where Jessica was wrapping fragile purchases. "Kevin. Ian texted that he needs a water bottle in the movie room. He said he's given the tour intro so many times his throat is dry."

"Sure thing. I ran out of stickers though. Got any more?"

She glanced at the clock on the wall. "Don't worry about it. Holly told me to close tours at four. Anyone else that comes in before five will either visit the gift shop or wait until tomorrow."

Kevin nodded. "I'll get that water, then." He shuffled through the maze of people until he reached the doors to the back offices, picking up his pace. Once he reached the small fridge and grabbed a water, he turned to leave when Holly burst in.

"Kevin?"

Holly stopped so fast when she spotted Kevin that her upper body lurched forward. "I've been looking for you."

Kevin froze as their eyes locked. "Sorry I was late. I visited Nick first. I wasn't thinking about how busy you'd be." He broke the gaze and tilted his head toward the gift shop. "Looks like you had an outstanding day."

Holly stepped forward, her smile widening as she reached him. "You have no idea. I have so much to tell you. For starters, I need to apologize for all the terrible things I said. I didn't mean any of it."

He held up the water bottle. "I know. It's okay. I really want to talk to you, too. Ian needs this water. Where can we meet?"

She clicked her tongue at the thought. "Rachel wanted to show me a snow scene she has set up. It's in the hallway upstairs. She secured former displays from Macy's store fronts and is working on an idea to have fake snow fall as guests walk through. Do you want to deliver Ian's water and find me there?"

"Sounds great." He sprinted off with a whistle.

Holly felt hope surge throughout her as she took the stairs to the new exhibit. *Thank You, God. Uncle Nick's recovering. The mansion had a successful Black Friday. Kevin's still talking to me. You're amazing. Thank You for Your love and grace.* She pushed the heavy metal door open to find *Marshmallow World* playing through hallway speakers. A light snow started as soon as she stepped into the hall.

Rachel waved from the other end of the hall and glided toward her, a huge smile pasted on her face as she reached Holly. "What do you think? The service fraternity at school helped build it all."

Holly faced the first window. An oversized suspended globe with the words "Christmas Around the World" danced in front of her. Below the globe was a telescope with a group of animated children in line. One child stood on tip-toes, the telescope roving back and forth displaying an airplane over an ocean. Then a small train rolling on tracks. Finally, a cab parked next to a storefront. "Rachel." Words caught in Holly's throat. "It's stunning."

Rachel exhaled. "It gets better. C'mon."

Holly visited each window dedicated to a different county and a child's Christmas experience. Germany. France. England.

United States. Each window had holiday music for that country. The electronics, the Santa listening to a small little girl in the American display while animated elves dashed around the store aisles crossing off her list, it was nothing short of magical. She struggled to find the words to convey to Rachel how amazing this was. "I never could have managed these changes and upgrades without all of your help. If I could give you each a college degree for what you've done for The Christmas Mansion, I would."

Rachel stayed silent for a moment, taking Holly's hand and leading her to the very end of the windows. A decorated Christmas tree stood in the corner with a wider than usual base. "Kevin and his students built this for you."

Holly bent down to examine the tree base. There was a slit in the front. "What's this?"

"Read the sign."

Holly straightened and peered at the placard on the wall. "Please place donations in base of tree to honor the memory of Chris Christmas and to help The Christmas Mansion become debt-free." She put her hand over her mouth and shook her head. Before she could respond, the door on her side of the hall opened. Kevin.

"You found the tree." He turned toward Holly.

She slowly nodded. "I found a lot of things recently. Do you want to go with me to the hospital to visit Uncle Nick? We need to talk."

Chapter Twenty-Three

Kevin tilted his head as he watched Holly and Nick trade laughs. In their hour visit with him, Holly hadn't run out of stories about her Black Friday experience at the mansion. Her favorite being the five-year-old who wanted his mom to bring him there for a tour every single day. The crying baby that saw suspended ornaments in the guest room and settled down. The bossy big sister that got stuck in Santa's chimney and the little brother had to guide her out. Holly's face glowed as she spoke.

Nick reached for his cup of water on the bed stand and took a sip. "Your father would be so proud. He always was. But these last few months, Holly, what you've accomplished at the mansion is fantastic."

Holly's face beamed. "Uncle Nick, it was all the students. And Kevin. The college group and Kevin's class had amazing ideas and made them happen. Now the challenge is to keep everything in working condition for our community celebration."

Kevin swallowed hard as he focused on her black leggings and toned muscles. "You have about ten days, right? We'll help."

Nick nodded. "That's right. We'll all work together."

Holly held up a hand. "Wait a minute. I appreciate the thought, but Uncle Nick, you need to focus on your recovery."

The senior citizen rolled his eyes. "My plan is to put on the Santa costume and listen to kids share their Christmas wishes. Easy."

She chuckled. "Uh-huh. You forget the stress that comes with crying babies. Moms who want the perfect picture."

Kevin checked his watch and stood. "My guess is the doctors will be very clear with him on what he's allowed and not allowed to do." He turned toward his pretty lady, wearing a blue dress. "Hey, gorgeous woman in blue, visiting hours are almost over. How about I treat you to dinner?"

She reached for her purse and rose. "Okay. But I'll be back tomorrow."

The tired-looking older man clicked on the television. "You two don't worry about me. This is one of the busiest weeks of the year for the mansion. Do what you need to do. I'll be right here watching westerns."

Holly bent down and gave her uncle a kiss on the cheek. "You're just like Daddy. Please do what they tell you."

He nodded and pushed a button on the remote. "Have something greasy for me."

Kevin laughed as he opened the door for Holly. "Will do, Sir."

Thirty minutes later, Kevin sat across from Holly in the Mt. Morris diner, staring at their cups of coffee. *I need a distraction from those gorgeous eyes. The shapely legs. How her dress hangs in all the right places.* He reached for his cup and nearly squeezed the hot liquid out with his grip. "Nick has his color back in his cheeks. I think that's a good sign."

She nodded as she traced her finger along the white mug bearing the diner logo. "I'm afraid he'll overdo it when he gets home."

"Not with us around. We'll watch out for him."

Holly raised her eyebrows. "Us."

He cleared his throat and reached for her hand. "I like how it sounds."

She laced her fingers with his. "I have so much to share. I wanted you to be the first to know something happened Thanksgiving night. I went to the chapel and I had an experience. A breakthrough, perhaps."

Kevin straightened, ready to move next to her, wrap his arms around her and pull her close until a server dropped a glass and brought him back to his senses. "What happened?"

She sighed. “There was such a pit in my stomach. I was scared for Uncle Nick. Upset that I hurt you so deeply. I was drawn to the chapel. I met the chaplain and he listened to me. I confessed how sorry I was for resenting the mansion and Christmas when I was growing up. How I miss my parents. That I pushed you away and regretted it because I love you—”

Kevin narrowed his gaze. “What did you say?”

“I love you. It’s scary because I don’t know what will happen. But my prayer is God will direct us.”

He dropped her hand and reached for a napkin, wiping the moisture off. “Holly?”

She placed her arms on the Formica table and grinned. “The chaplain explained God’s grace to me. His love through His Son, Jesus. I carried an emotional anchor around thanks to my mistakes and sin, yet, I am lovely to God. He is crazy about me. The sensation I have from all God has for me pulses through me, Kevin. There’s so much I sense inside of me that I never did before. Peace. There’s so much peace now.”

Kevin lowered his head. “This is all an answer to prayer. Nathan’s going to fly to the North Pole without a sleigh he’ll be so excited.”

“What about you?”

Kevin played with the napkin, ripping up a little piece off the corner. “What about me?”

“Are you able to forgive me for keeping you at arm’s length?” She bit her lip as she waited.

He took a sip of the warm, mild coffee. “I forgave you last night. Uncle Nick had a lot of wisdom to share.”

Her eyes twinkled against the drab décor. “I’m sure he did. So, what now?”

Kevin chuckled. “That’s easy. Let’s put our trust in Him as we explore us.”

"Us." The curve in Holly's mouth turned up as she kept repeating. "Us. I like the sound of it."

Ten days later, Holly gazed into the full-length mirror and turned in her Kelly-green dress. *Okay God, I need Your strength. I'm nervous. The media and everyone from Geneseo Valley is coming out for our celebration tonight. I want them to fall in love with The Christmas Mansion.* She reached for her barrettes and bobby pins to work on the bun she wanted to create. "'Father, that everyone would fall in love with Your Son's birthday. And the mansion." Holly blew out a shaky breath. She still didn't know what she would say in live interviews, or how visitors would respond to their tour, but peace filled her.

The doorbell rang, and Holly shoved the last pin in to secure her hair. "Coming!" She slowly maneuvered the stairs since she wasn't used to wearing heels. Once she reached the peephole, Kevin's glasses were the first thing Holly noticed. "You look like you belong on a cover of a fancy men's magazine."

Kevin stepped through the entrance and chuckled. "It's the suit and the glasses. Makes me look like a GQ cover model, right?" He bent down to give her a kiss on the cheek. "We should leave. You don't want to be late for your own party."

Holly's stomach lurched when they arrived at the mansion twenty minutes later. The parking lot was full and a line already was forming to get inside. She inhaled slowly, then exhaled. "I can do all things through Christ. I can do all things through Christ."

Kevin turned off the engine and faced her, placing his hand on her cheek, caressing it with his thumb. "Holly Christmas, you've got this. You were born to show families the wonder of the season here at the mansion."

She nodded with closed eyes and faster breathing.

Kevin drew closer and planted a kiss that bloomed into an embrace. Her knees began shaking. “Okay. That felt more like the Fourth of July. But I’m not complaining.” She winked.

He opened the door. “Let’s do this.”

The next two hours were abuzz with Adam, Ian and Rachel leading tours. Uncle Nick sat in the oversized red chair and played Santa. Kevin’s class monitored the guest room by making sure no one got stuck in Santa’s chimney. Jessica worked the register. Kevin assisted guests in the gift shop. Holly absorbed it all as the cameraman attached a lapel mic to her dress.

“I haven’t been here since I was a little girl. You’ve done an amazing job bringing it up-to-date so the new generation can enjoy it here, too.” Regan Quinn, the Rochester-area reporter who covered Livingston County events, checked her phone.

“Thank you. The Christmas Mansion is about making happy memories for families.”

Regan looked to the cameraman, who gave her a thumb’s up. He returned to his equipment while she took her microphone. “Let’s work on spreading the word so many can take you up on that, shall we?”

Ten minutes later, Holly followed Regan’s cue as the anchor desk announced they were about to visit the mansion live. The blond reporter smiled and faced the camera. “Fred, Roxanne, I’m here at The Christmas Mansion where Holly Christmas and her elves have unveiled a beautiful update for families of all ages to enjoy. Holly, it’s obvious the mansion is a passion for you and your family, starting with your parents decades ago. Why keep such a big place operating when Christmas is so commercial and families opt for bigger cities and fancier tourist destinations?”

Holly smiled. “I love Christmas. I want everyone to experience the merriment and wonder as they travel through our new exhibits. If families are considering a holiday tradition, or want to return to one they remember from their own childhoods, The

Christmas Mansion is the place to be." She glanced at Kevin, who gave her a double thumbs up as he mouthed *I love you*. Her stomach felt like one of the snow globes, shook to the core. She winked and mouthed it back. *God, You are good. Thank You for every blessing from above.*

Regan paused. "Last question. Would you be willing to show viewers the guest room? Rumor has it there is Santa's chimney."

Holly nodded. "It's true. You're welcome to try it." She gestured the cameraman to follow them as their heels clicked the short distance. Regan used the mic the entire time, but gasped as soon as she saw the suspended ornaments. "This is magical."

Holly nodded as the impact of those three words hit her. The Christmas Mansion was no longer the source of her resentment or an albatross hanging around her neck forcing her to return to Geneseo Valley. It was truly as Regan described. Magical.

Chapter Twenty-Four

Kevin paced Jonah's kitchen, holding the velvet box in his hand. "Am I crazy?"

Jonah chuckled and poured himself a glass of orange juice. "You don't want me to really answer that, do you?"

Kevin looked at the time. "I have to leave for work. I definitely don't want to be late on Valentine's Day."

"I'll be praying for you." Jonah tipped his glass in salute.

Two hours later, Kevin parked the school van and counted heads as the students scrambled out and made their way to the mansion entrance. Nathan was the last to leave the vehicle, a huge smile on his maturing face. The grin had a hint of mischief to it, so Kevin gestured for the boy to join him. "Anything going on I should know about?"

Nathan rolled his eyes and laughed. "You love Valentine's Day."

Kevin pursed his lips. *Sometimes it takes time to see where Nathan's going with his thinking*. "Okay, is that what's making you so happy?"

Nathan's face was expressionless. "You love Christmas."

Kevin watched the other unchaperoned kids fill the gift shop. *Who knows what could be broken*. "Nathan, I love the holidays. Can we get to work and not get in trouble?"

"You love Holly Christmas." Nathan giggled and ran to catch up with his friends.

Kevin looked around to see if anyone heard the exchange.

Holly stepped into view. "I see Nathan's in rare form today."

He jammed his hands in his pockets and felt the small velvet box. "Maybe Cupid shot him with an arrow. As long as he doesn't break anything, I'm okay with it."

She chuckled and laid a hand on his arm. "One thing I learned quickly about Nathan, he tells it like he sees it. Months ago he knew I hated Christmas." Holly glanced around the room. "Everything's changed. God used him to heal my heart, and bring you into my life."

Kevin swallowed hard. *There's no way I'm going to be able to keep this box in my pocket until our dinner.* "I'm so grateful for all He's done for us." Out of the corner of his eye he noticed Nathan trotting behind the counter with Uncle Nick. "I hate to stop this moment, but we should put the students to work."

Holly nodded and entered the gift shop. "Who's ready to make Valentines? We're having a sale tonight for a couple hours. Every family that visits gets a coupon, a chocolate sample, and a homemade valentine."

A dozen hands raised, some students using both arms. Kevin shook his head and gestured for the kids to follow him to the conference room. "I need each of you to use your neatest handwriting."

He counted heads again and realized someone was missing. Nathan. He glanced down the hall and spotted Holly, alone.

"Everything okay? I thought I left plenty of construction paper, markers, and colored pencils."

Kevin kept his focus on the hallway. "Did you see Nathan?"

She smiled. "He's still at the counter chatting with Uncle Nick. Should I get him?"

Suddenly, the senior citizen and the tween appeared, heading toward the conference room. Nathan was carrying a heart-shaped box.

Kevin stepped toward them. "Nathan, what's going on?"

Nathan thrust the red package in Holly's hands. "Happy Valentine's Day. It's chocolate."

Holly nodded. "That's so sweet. Thank you, Nathan—"

The tween reached over and lifted the top off. “Kevin loves you and wants to marry you.”

Kevin coughed as he saw the ring he planned to present to Holly later in the evening sitting on the center square of the chocolates. “Nathan! Where did you get that?”

Holly’s eyes widened. “What’s going on?”

Nick’s chuckle grew into a full laugh. Kevin turned and realized the entire class left their seats and were watching their every move as Nick raised his hand. “I’m afraid I’m to take some blame. Nathan confessed he saw the box this morning on the counter and he figured out you were going to propose.”

Holly gasped and put her hands to her mouth.

“He asked me to pick up a box of candy on the way here this morning. I didn’t know he was going to put your ring in it. I thought he was going to make you give her some milk chocolate at dinner. Don’t be mad. It’s a sweet idea.” Nick’s eyes twinkled.

Nathan raised his eyebrows as he faced Kevin. “What? You love her. You want to marry her.”

Kevin looked to the boy, who remained steadfast in his assessment. He glanced to his other side, and saw Holly standing in place, her focus on the ring. “I don’t even know who to talk to first.”

“Holly.” Uncle Nick and Nathan spoke together.

“Me.” Holly’s light voice followed.

Kevin slowly nodded and reached for the ring. Giggles filled the hallway when he bent on one knee. “Nathan’s right. I love you, Holly Christmas and I want to spend the rest of my life with you. Will you marry me?” His hand shook as he held up the ring.

“Oh, Kevin. I love you, too. You’re God’s gift to me. I would love to be your wife.” She looked to Uncle Nick and squealed.

Kevin reached for her hand and slid the ring on her finger. “Nathan isn’t the only one working with Nick.” He cleared his throat as Holly tilted her head. “Sweetheart, this is your mother’s ring.”

The students couldn't remain quiet or still for another moment. Before she could respond, both of them were slammed together by a group hug, then applause, followed by high-fives and squeals. Kevin reached for her and squeezed her hands.

Nathan was the first to back away, and the rest followed. "This is the best day ever. When will you get married?"

Kevin stepped closer to Holly and nudged her, while she giggled. The two exchanged glances and looked to the class of excited students. "Christmas."

If You Enjoyed Restoring Christmas...

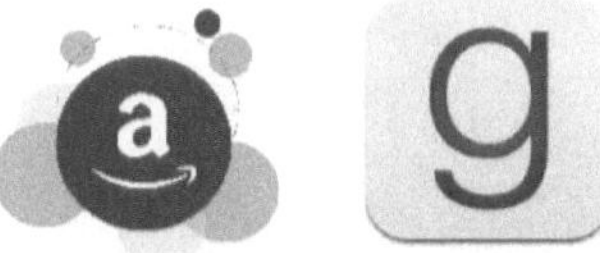

It would mean a lot if you would leave a review. The more reviews a book receives, the more attention Amazon gives the book. Reviews don't need to be long. Thank you!

You can also follow Julie Arduini on Amazon and Goodreads so you'll be the first to know when a new book releases.

About Restoring Christmas

Restoring Christmas first came to light when I joined the *Christmas to Remember* boxed set team in late 2017. After visiting the real life tourist attraction Castle Noel in Medina, Ohio, the plot came to life. What if the heroine was part of a Christmas family business and hated the holiday?

I love Christmas now, but there was a brief time as a teen it triggered dread and panic. I remembered previous family events that were not festive. Thankfully, as I surrendered my past, present and future to Christ, He healed my pain and gave me reason to celebrate.

If you struggle with grief, especially during the Christmas season, know that your Heavenly Father weeps and mourns with you. Jesus will turn your sorrow to rejoicing. Please know I am praying for you, and that your healing come sooner than later.

Acknowledgements

-Thank you to the beautiful village of Geneseo (Jen-ah-see-o) and the State University of New York at Geneseo for giving me a wonderful college experience and a backdrop to set this story. Geneseo Valley is based on Geneseo.

-The Christmas House in Elmira, NY. I loved visiting there as a teen and the memories helped me envision The Christmas Mansion.

-Castle Noel in Medina, OH. This spontaneous visit in November 2017 was so fun, such an overload for my senses and wonder that it was where the idea for a story started. What if someone worked at a Christmas-themed attraction and hated the holiday?

-Kimberly, thank you for letting me participate in the boxed set that made this story possible. It was my heart's desire to one day be part of a Christmas collaboration.

-Elizabeth and Valerie, for all your hard work behind the scenes for the beautiful 2018 boxed set experience.

-Lizz, thank you for your friendship, love, prayers, and for that life-changing photo shoot.

-To Scribes 202 and 210 for their critiques, Kim for her love of editing as a hobby, and Julie as my faithful proofreader. Laura Hilton, thank you for the title!

-Brenda, Kara, Ruth, Shirley, Tracie, Summer, Deb, Rita, Amy, Noreen: Thank you for covering me, my family, and writing in prayer.

-The Shetsky Family. Regan will not be forgotten. The news reporter Regan Quinn was named to remember her and honor Kelly's former career.

-Pastor Gary Gray for allowing me to use anything from his sermons. Every life is redeemable comes from a sermon and is one of our core values.

-Mom, Crista, and Landon. The celery and cream cheese will always be our family tradition.

-Tom, Brian, and Hannah. Thanks for the space and grace you gave as I holed up and wrote while you ate burned lasagna and tacos, again. The pumpkin pies and blueberries mentioned were for you.

-To Jesus, who is Christmas and the Restorer of my heart and soul. Every word I write is for Your glory.

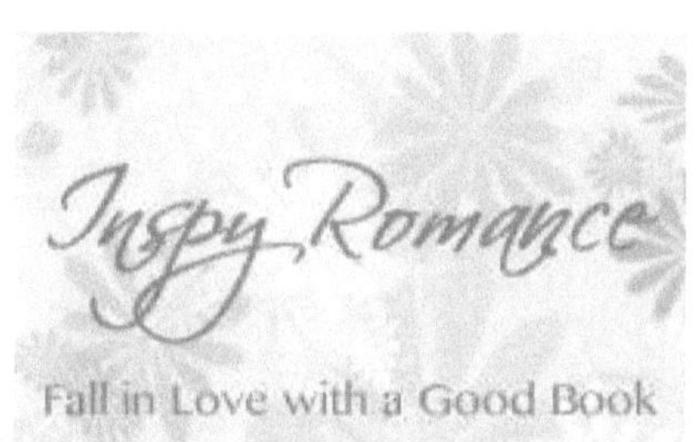

Inspy Romance
Fall in Love with a Good Book

Follow Julie Arduini and other Inspy Romance authors:

Blog:

http://inspyromance.com

Twitter:

http://twitter.com/inspyromance

Facebook:

http://facebook.com/inspyromance

Pinterest:

http://pinterest.com/inspyromance

Follow Julie Arduini and other Christian authors at Christians Read.

Blog:

http://christiansread.wordpress.com

Facebook:

http://facebook.com/christiansread

Twitter:

http://twitter.com/christiansread

Looking for
an Encouraging Speaker?

Julie Arduini is passionate about encouraging audiences to find freedom through surrender. She's able to speak on a wide range of surrender topics, the writing process, family, motherhood, and her own books.

Learn more by contacting her at
juliearduini@juliearduini.com

.

Regan's Acts of Kindness

Although I never met Regan, her parents spent a lot of time with our family when we lived in Upstate NY. Regan was taken from them in January 2017. She would have turned five in March.

Everyone who loved Regan wants her to be remembered.

Here are different ways you can help make that happen:

Like Regan's Acts of Kindness on Facebook and participate. http://facebook.com/RegansActsofKindness

Paint Rocks and Hide them in appropriate places in your community. Check the Facebook page above to learn how to tag them to keep the kindness flowing.

Visit Regan's Corner at The Wild Animal Park in Chittenango, New York http://thewildpark.com

Other Books by Julie Arduini

If you enjoyed *Restoring Christmas*, you might enjoy *Entrusted.*

Jenna Anderson leaves her Ohio hometown for the unknown in Speculator Falls. She's determined to make her new job as senior center work and become one of the locals. Ben Regan's family is the backbone of Speculator Falls and he's made a vow to protect the rural village. When his grandfather passes away and his former girlfriend leaves without even saying goodbye, Ben's determined to prevent further transition in his life. But Jenna produces a lot of change for Ben in a book about surrendering the present fears we have about change and wanting to belong.

Contemporary Romance
The Surrendering Time Series:
Entrusted:
https://www.amazon.com/gp/product/B01FGC1Z8W
Entangled:
https://www.amazon.com/gp/product/B01FG7JALG
Engaged
https://www.amazon.com/gp/product/B072K91W25
Finding Freedom Through Surrender: 30-Day Devotional featuring characters and themes from the Surrendering Time series:
https://www.amazon.com/gp/product/B06XBHM2P3

Stand-Alone Christian Romance
Match Made in Heaven
https://www.amazon.com/Match-Made-Heaven-Julie-Arduini-ebook/dp/B07QR29X51/

Surrendering Stinkin' Thinkin' Series with Hannah Arduini:

You're Beautiful:

https://www.amazon.com/gp/product/B078VK3JJB

You're Amazing

https://www.amazon.com/Youre-Amazing-Surrendering-Stinkin-Thinkin-ebook/dp/B07M7D6HSV

You're Brilliant (Coming Winter 2020)

A Walk in the Valley Infertility Devotional Workbook with Heidi Glick, Elizabeth Maddrey, Kym McNabney, Paula Mowery and Donna Winters

https://www.amazon.com/Walk-Valley-Christian-encouragement-infertility-ebook/dp/B06XC36GMV

About the Author

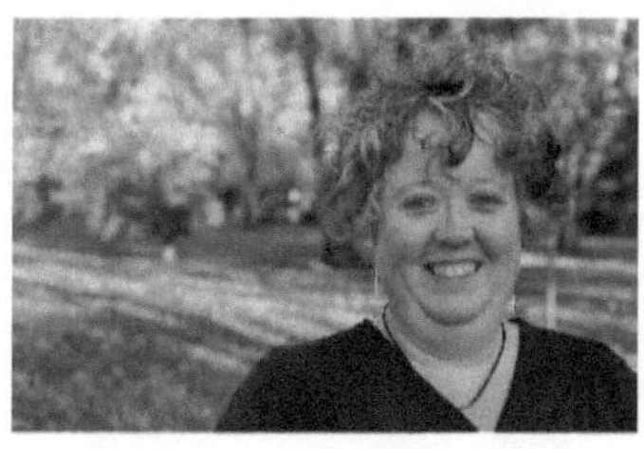

Julie Arduini loves to encourage readers to find freedom in Christ by surrendering the good, the bad, and ---maybe one day---the chocolate. She's the author of the contemporary romance series SURRENDERING TIME, (Entrusted, Entangled, Engaged,) as well as the stand-alone novellas, MATCH MADE IN HEAVEN and RESTORING CHRISTMAS. She also shares her story in the infertility devotional, A WALK IN THE VALLEY. Her other latest release, YOU'RE AMAZING, is a book for girls ages 10-100, written with her teenaged daughter, Hannah, and is book 2 in their SURRENDERING STINKIN' THINKIN' series. She blogs every other Wednesday for Christians Read, as well as monthly with Inspy Romance. She resides in Ohio with her husband and two children. Learn more by visiting her at http://juliearduini.com, where she invites readers to opt in to her content full of resources and giveaway opportunities.

www.ingramcontent.com/pod-product-compliance
Lightning Source LLC
Chambersburg PA
CBHW030313130626
46549CB00002B/828

* 9 7 8 1 7 3 3 6 8 7 6 2 1 *